THE STONE HOUSE

D1150617

C334016629

CLASS

CREATED BY
PATRICK NESS

THE STONE HOUSE

A.K. BENEDICT

1 3 5 7 9 10 8 6 4 2

BBC Books, an imprint of Ebury Publishing
20 Vauxhall Bridge Road,
London SW1V 2SA

BBC Books is part of the Penguin Random House group of companies
whose addresses can be found at global.penguinrandomhouse.com

Penguin
Random House
UK

Copyright © A.K. Benedict 2016

A.K. Benedict has asserted her right to be identified as the author of this
Work in accordance with the Copyright, Designs and Patents Act 1988

This book is published to accompany the television series entitled *Class* first
broadcast on BBC Three in 2016. *Class* is a BBC Wales production.

Executive producers: Patrick Ness, Steven Moffat and Brian Minchin

First published by BBC Books in 2016

www.penguin.co.uk

A CIP catalogue record for this book is available from the British Library

ISBN 9781785941870

Printed and bound in Great Britain by Clays Ltd, St Ives PLC

Penguin Random House is committed to a sustainable future for
our business, our readers and our planet. This book is made from
Forest Stewardship Council® certified paper.

MIX
Paper from
responsible sources
FSC® C018179
www.fsc.org

To James, Guy and
Dame Margaret Rutherford

CHAPTER ONE

HELP ME

You know that abandoned house round the corner? Garden rammed with dandelions, weeds reaching through the gates like gnarled hands? Stay away. No, really, STAY AWAY. It wants the lonely, the lost, the vulnerable. It wants you.

If *I'd* stayed away, I'd be home right now doing normal evening-type stuff like eating Shreddies from the packet and hacking the Pentagon. Instead, I'm trapped inside the stone house, screaming at the cobwebbed glass. I know, I know, I was warned. 'Don't go near,' Mum said. She didn't say why. Why doesn't anyone say why? It's all meaningful looks and 'take my word for it', not facts. I like facts. Facts, I can handle. Facts such as 'some snails have hairy shells'. That's a good fact. You can hold on to facts like hair clings

1

to the shell of the *Trochulus hispidus*. If you don't have facts then fiction slips in.

Rumours cling to this house like ivy but what's inside is far worse. Its halls are stalked by nightmares, its nightmares stalked by whatever is keeping me here. If you see me at the window, send help. We don't have much time. The stone house is alive and growing more powerful. Whatever you do, stay away. It'll never let you go.

CHAPTER TWO

DANDELIONS

Three days earlier...

Tanya leans against Coal Hill's gates. Ram's late. He said he'd be out of training by five. It's now twenty past and hot. Unseasonably hot, even for the time of year. The kind of hot that makes you check for sweat patches. The kind of hot where sweat patches join forces into one giant sweat patchwork. The kind of hot where you definitely don't want to be waiting to help someone else with his homework. But he'd insisted she talk it through with him on the way home. And, typically, having made the plan, a plan she'd dropped everything for, he's forgotten all about it.

Tanya kicks at one of the dandelion clocks growing through the cracks in the pavement. Its seeds scatter. There were already lots in the air, carried by a slight breeze. She picks another at the base of the stem and holds its fuzzy white head to her lips. It takes three puffs to disperse: three o'clock. Not even close. Some clock.

A stray seed brushes her cheek. Others land in her hair, just in her line of vision. She picks it out and examines it. It's kind of cute. It looks like a tiny umbrella, spokes splayed. She looks it up. Turns out they're called filamentous achenes. Fancy name for a seed. She'll call it Brian.

Minutes pass. Still nothing back from Ram. Bet he's forgotten or bumped into someone more important. She sends another message: 'I'm off'.

Tanya walks away, squinting into the sun. She's broken her new sunglasses. Again. Lucky they were only a fiver at the market. She sat on them while arguing what should have been a winning point with Charlie. It kind of undermines your case when you jump up and say 'arsecakes'. Miss Quill said that she wasn't to use that particular argument in the exam. Tanya doesn't have much luck with sunglasses. She has no idea how Ram manages to keep his designer ones pristine, no idea how he, or anyone else, achieves pristine anything. Too much effort. She's seen April with the Nair tube, watched with a mixture of horror and fascination as the egg-sandwich-scented cream made the hairs crinkle up and shrug away from the skin.

A long way off, an ice-cream van sings. It's a welcome sound but if the last term has taught her anything it's that you can't trust innocuous things like ice cream. What kind of alien would drive an ice-cream van? One that needs a cover story and easy access to ice – a snow monster who toppled through the bunghole. She never used to think like this. Everything is now possible, other than Ram turning up on time.

Tanya looks around, then slowly turns 360 degrees. This isn't the right estate. Towels and geraniums, flags and clothes hang outside flats but she doesn't recognise any of them. Mrs Cartwright's Collie usually meets her with a lick by the playground but this is a different playground. An indifferent tabby flicks its tail across hot tarmac.

She's gone the wrong way. Somehow her feet have taken her in the other direction, through another estate, other streets. Feet do that. Stupid feet. It must be the heat. Now she'll have to circle round. Always go forwards, even if it's to go back. There's only one way, unless she wants to go by the canal and the only reason to go there is if you want a spare shopping trolley, tetanus or to play Count the Condoms. The other way, though, will take her down a certain street on which a certain building stands. It'll be fine, Tanya tells herself as she rounds the corner. You're being silly. It's only an old stone house.

CHAPTER THREE

RUMOURS

The house stands on its own at the end of the road. It must be at least eighteenth century and looks old and incongruous next to the divided terraces and posh new-build apartments, as out of time and place as if it had been lifted up by an unlikely London tornado and plonked down in an East End street. She'd probably find the withered limbs of a local witch sticking out from underneath if she dug around in the rose bushes. Three storeys high, peeling purple and grey paint on stone – it's the kind of house the Addams Family would shake their heads at, telling the estate agent, 'It's not for us, bit too *gothic.*'

If the rumours are true then kids have visited and gone missing, that others have died. You'd think that'd make it the perfect place for teenagers to dare and date each other but most stay away. Last time Tanya was here, she'd stepped inside the porch and felt so cold and alone that she ran out and didn't come back. Until now.

It's one of those places that rumours stick to like filamentous achenes to your hair. It can't be that bad. And it looks like it's going to find another owner, at last. There's a SOLD sign in the front garden, weeds growing up to its hips. The rusting gates have been unlocked as well, although you can still hardly see the path running up to the front door.

Trees loom in the back garden, placing the pavement in front of the house into shadow. It feels like the only cool space in London. She feels an urge to sit down in the grass, disappearing from view of the road. She'd better get home, though. Homework to do.

As Tanya walks away, she sees something move in a window. Getting closer to the railings, she looks up. In the top left window, a face presses against the glass. A young woman. Her fists hit at the window but make no sound. Her mouth opens in a silent scream.

CHAPTER FOUR

THE GIRL IN THE WINDOW

She saw me. I know she did. Most people walk by quickly, never looking up and even if they do, their eyes skim over me. They don't want to look at my face. They don't want to know. But she wasn't afraid, not in the way they are. I shouted out to her and she stared straight at me. Even when she was walking away, she kept looking back, looking at ME. I could cry. I am crying and I thought I didn't have any more tears left.

I'd like a friend. I used to have friends in Damascus, and then there were kind people who helped me on the long journey here. Now I only have the house and its nightmares. I used to think I was really lucky. I had a wonderful time up to the age of eight or nine, living with Baba, Ummi and Yana when she was a toddler, all grabby hands and baby-teeth smile. I went to school and was a good scholar, particularly at English. Baba taught me how to get plants to grow from a seed and dance towards the light and Yana planted her dolls upside down, saying their long hair were roots.

That was before the war affected everything, and then luck turned against me, whispered when my back was turned and now I am here, alone. I mustn't wish the girl back. If she does return, she might catch my bad luck. She might never leave. Like me.

CHAPTER FIVE

IT'S ALL A MATTER OF PRACTICE

The knife gleams in Miss Quill's hand. She sharpens it even more then turns the handle in her hands. It's heavy, made from rare Kalthagon stone that reacts to body temperature. She aims it at the black paper silhouette attached to the back door.

The front door opens. Charlie and Matteusz walk in, laughing.

The knife zings into the silhouette's head.

'That'd hurt,' Charlie says.

'Certainly sting,' Matteusz replies.

'Definite inconvenience,' says Charlie, walking over to the fridge.

'I'm practising,' she says. 'Distractions are not welcome.' Placing the knife back in its sheath, she takes a larger knife from the leather case and polishes it.

'You could keep your knife throwing to the bedroom,' Charlie says. 'Wait, that doesn't sound right.'

'The kitchen is the place for knives,' Miss Quill says.

'It's just that it's not the most relaxing thing to come home to,' Charlie says. He takes out the vat of orange juice and pours two glasses.

'When we're no longer in mortal danger from an inter-planetary or inter-dimensional threat, then I won't practise in the kitchen,' Miss Quill says.

'That'll be never, then.' Charlie hands one of the glasses to Matteusz and follows him to the stairs. 'We're going to start on the small mountain of homework you gave us, then we're going out.'

'Next time it'll be a mountain range,' Miss Quill says.

Miss Quill puts the kettle on. She has papers to mark and classes to prepare and perpetual darkness to fight. She's going to need coffee.

Upstairs, she hears them walk across Charlie's bedroom. A chair is scraped across the floor, a thump of a textbook on the floor. The surprising thing, given her experience, is that they *do* actually study after school. She's passed an open door and seen them lying on the floor, books open, pens poised. Unless they are very quick at moving when they hear her coming up the stairs. She's not sure what she'd rather – scholastic diligence or deception skills. Both are useful in warfare.

She can hear them laughing, even over the boiling kettle. He smiles so much more now. He's too relaxed. Relationships do not further any cause, they diminish your fight, make you less strong by yourself. She pours hot water onto the ground coffee and watches it swirl. There's an expression here for what it feels like to fall for someone: 'go weak at the knees'. Why would you want to be weak anywhere?

The young people in her charge are so young and full of optimism and need to cling to each other. Not her. She doesn't need family or memories or anything that holds her back. All she needs is coffee and the means to fight.

She throws the large knife at the silhouette. And another. Two more. Each knife finds a place in its heart. Not that it has one. Shadows don't have hearts.

CHAPTER SIX

THE EARLY HOURS

Tanya stares at her ceiling. It's 4 a.m. She's hardly slept. In theory that means she's grabbed bits of non-REM sleep but not enough to be rested. She should know, she's spent hours reading up on the sleep she isn't having. Not that she can concentrate. She can't stop thinking of the girl in the window. She's probably got it wrong, she must have. What if the girl wasn't saying 'help', but 'hello' instead? It's within the realms of possibility, and these days those realms are gargantuan.

She turns on her side, facing the window. The light is already pressing against the curtains. She'll wait till six. That's an almost OK time, isn't it? Ram'll probably already be up by then, squatting and flexing. She sets an alarm on her phone. Maybe she can get just a little bit of sleep. The outline of the stone house window flashes against her eyes when she closes them.

Several hours later, Tanya's in the classroom with Charlie, Matteusz and April, half an hour early for class. Not even nine in the morning and it's already hot. It's lasted for more than a day so obviously the media have declared it a heatwave.

Charlie and Matteusz are looking at something on a phone.

'Go on then,' April says. 'You said it was important.'

'I'm waiting for Ram,' Tanya says. 'He said he'd be here.' It took an hour of begging and wheedling over DM but he'd promised in the end.

Ten minutes later, Ram ambles through the door.

'Nice of you to join us,' Charlie says.

'Isn't it,' Ram replies. 'I'd rather be doing anything else at all but, no, I'm stuck inside with you.'

'Charming,' Tanya says. She then tells them what happened last night, right up to seeing the face at the window.

'How could you see that from where you were standing?' April asks.

It's a reasonable question. She'd ask it herself if she hadn't been there. But she had been. And that's what she saw. 'I just could,' she says.

'You said it was shadowed,' April says, 'and it *was* very hot yesterday.'

Tanya bites back rising anger. 'I didn't make it up.'

April shrugs. She's got one of those little battery-operated fans that don't do much. It's got a reassuring whir and wafts her hair. She has very waftable hair.

'No one's saying that,' Ram says, leaning back in his chair. 'Not exactly, anyway. We're implying it.'

'What did the police say?' Matteusz asks, paying attention at last.

Tanya sighed. 'They said they'd send someone round. They hadn't by the time I'd left. I waited as long as I could. I had to go home at some point.' She knew she was justifying it to the girl left in the house, not to them. Tanya had gone back this morning and stood outside the stone house. It felt as if it was calling to her, pulling her in. It felt sad down to every stone. There was no sign of the girl in the window. She could still be there, trapped in that room. 'I'm going back after school today. Come with me, you'll see.'

'I can't tonight,' April says, checking her diary. 'Got two committee meetings.'

Charlie and Matteusz look at each other. Matteusz bites his lip.

'You're trying to think of a reason why you can't go, aren't you?' Tanya says.

Charlie shrugs. 'You saw someone in the window of a house. It's hardly invading alien levels of panic.'

Tanya's certainty begins to slip. 'I'm not saying it's life or death. Not yet, anyway.'

'I'm just thinking there's plenty going on without looking for trouble,' Charlie says.

'I'm not looking for trouble, I'm just – never mind. What about you, Ram? What's your excuse this time?'

Miss Quill bustles through the door. 'What are you doing here?' she asks. 'Has April infected you with slightly unsightly keenness? Or have you all been replaced again? Tell me I don't have to find an authenticating gun at this time on a Tuesday morning.'

They all look to Tanya. Clearly it's her call on whether to tell her. 'We're just...' Tanya searches for a reason. Any reason. Nothing is coming. She doesn't want to tell her the truth. Miss Quill won't believe her any more than the others.

'Helping me with my homework, Miss Quill,' Ram says. 'I couldn't get the hang of it myself.'

Miss Quill stares at them all. 'If it's wrong then you've all got a problem with it,' she says. 'And we can go over the whole thing again.'

They groan.

'Can't you take it easy on us, Miss Quill?' Ram asks. 'It's too hot to think.'

'You think this is hot? Try thinking on the back of a fire stallion while riding through the flame lake of Kabal. Too hot to think indeed,' she mutters, taking out the textbook.

'We could find somewhere shady to work,' April suggests.

'What do you think this is, *Dead Poets Society*?' Miss Quill replies. 'You'd like that, wouldn't you. Do you think I'm going to lead you dancing through the underpass while you recite the underlying prames of the Renyalin series?'

'Don't you mean "primes"?' April replies.

'Don't get her started on prames,' Charlie whispers. 'We'll be here all day. They're from our planet. The prames of the Renyalin change according to weather, time and whoever is holding the aardvark.'

'What?' Ram says.

'I'll tell you later.'

'Do *I* get an aardvark?' Matteusz asks.

Charlie draws him a picture of an aardvark snorting ants through a rolled-up fiver.

'You're unusually quiet, Tanya,' Miss Quill says. She folds her arms and stares at Tanya, eyes flicking back and forth between her features. She looks like an owl seeking out a worm.

'I'm fine,' Tanya replies.

'If I've learned anything on this planet,' Miss Quill says, 'it's that "I'm fine" means anything but.'

'She's fine, Miss Quill,' April says. 'Really.' She adopts her bright, wide-eyed 'how could you not believe me?' face.

'In that case, why are you all bothering me? Don't you know it's hot?' Miss Quill says, fanning herself with the textbook.

CHAPTER SEVEN

STORM FRONT

After the last class, Ram is waiting for her at the entrance. 'You're late,' he says. 'If you're going to make me come with you then at least be on time.'

'But you *are* coming with me?' Tanya asks.

'Only so I can report back that there's nothing there.'

'Your confidence in me is touching.'

Ram leans against the railings, watching people leave.

'Do you never sweat?' she says. 'You look like you've fallen off the model conveyor. Stop it.'

'I could try, I suppose,' Ram says. Crinkling his brow only adds to the handsome.

'Shut up,' she says, leading them out of the grounds. They cross the road to the shady side of the street. If anything, the temperature has gone up. They weave through phalanxes of pushchairs and mums and dads complaining about how very 'close' it was, 'yes, very muggy', and that a 'storm is coming, mark my words'. To be fair, the sky has got that yellow, bad liver look that comes before a crashing thunderstorm.

Ram walks in front, swinging a tote bag. 'What's in the bag?' Tanya asks.

Ram hands it over. 'April made me take it.'

Tanya peers inside. There are two hand fans, two whistles, packets of biscuits, a torch, a compass, a portable charger and two apples. 'What do we need all this for?'

Ram shrugs. 'She said, "You never know".'

'I *do* know that I won't need a torch or a compass. Has she ever heard of apps?'

'We're lucky we got away with only this. She's got far more in her bag. Says it's better to be prepared than surprised.'

Tanya snorts. 'Yeah? What would you rather have, a surprise party or a preparation party?'

'April's got a preparation party planned for her surprise birthday party. That'll be fun,' Ram says.

'She's already prepared for her surprise party?'

'She's prepared the most surprised surprise birthday party face you'll ever see. She showed me. It's like this.' He raises his eyebrows as far as they can go, opens his mouth, eyes and nostrils wide. 'See? You've got to admit. That's good. I know, I've been looking in the mirror.'

'It's alright,' Tanya says. It's more than alright but he doesn't need to hear that.

'She says that if she wasn't prepared for it, she wouldn't look nearly as surprised.'

'That makes no sense whatsoever.'

'It does in April land.'

'Are there rides at April Land? Wait. Don't answer that,' Tanya says as they enter the estate.

Kids bellyflop over the swings, pushing with their feet, anything to get a breeze. That alien in an ice-cream van would make a killing here. The indifferent cat looks at her from the railings. It blinks once. Maybe it's beginning to like her. It jumps down and pisses on a patch of dandelions. Maybe not.

'It's this way, isn't it?' Ram says, pointing down a narrow alley.

'Have you been before?' Tanya asks.

'I went when I was a kid.'

'What were you doing there?'

Ram stops walking, hands on his hips. 'I know I said I'd come with you, but do we have to make small talk?'

'Tell me the story and I'll shut up,' Tanya says. 'Promise.'

'Fine,' he says, walking on. 'Some mates dared me to jump over the railings and go in. Everyone said a mad old woman lived there who used to pull out kids' teeth and make jewellery out of them.'

'I've seen something similar at Spitalfields market,' Tanya says. 'So what happened?'

'You said you'd shut up if I answered your question.'

'I said when you'd told me the story.'

'You really are a kid, aren't you? Wanting your bedtime story.' Ram sighs. 'Fine. You want to know, I'll tell you. Nothing much happened. I jumped over and had to wade through weeds to get to the front door. I was shorter then,' he says.

'Thanks for explaining how human growth works, Ram, it's a subject so few know anything about.'

'Right. Well, I reached my hand out for the door knocker and—'

'Why do all creepy houses have door knockers?' Tanya asks. 'Couldn't a few of them rig up a bell, just to make a change?'

'Stop interrupting. Do you want me to tell the story or not?'

'Sorry. No more interruptions. Carry on.'

'Right, well, I knocked on the door and it went "thud, thud, thud". Old-school horror. My mates were still on the other side of the gates, watching. I heard scuttling, close to the door. My heart was going for it, like I'd run from one goal line to the other. I didn't run away, though.' He was quiet then. They walked on. Tanya had to bite the side of her index finger to stop herself asking what happened.

'Aren't you going to ask what happened?' Ram asks.

'You're infuriating,' she says.

'I think we both know *that's* not true,' he says.

She considers for a moment. 'No,' she says, 'it really is.'

They stand on the street of the stone house. Their walking slows. 'The door opened,' Ram said, 'at which point my mates legged it. I should've run as well, only there was something that made me want to go in.'

'It felt like it was calling you?' Tanya asks.

'Exactly. So I stepped in. There's a sort of hallway, more like another room. Really big. Staircase going up to an open landing. Furniture, or something I didn't want to think about, covered in cloth. It was really dark, the windows so dirty that even without curtains it would've been impossible to see much. Cobwebs everywhere. I *could* tell though, that no one had opened the door. No one I could *see* anyway.'

The house is in sight. It looks even more isolated today. The grey of the stone house sits strangely against the blue sky and all the other houses seem as if they're edging away from it.

'Then what did you do?' Tanya asks. She wants Ram to keep talking, anything to take away the weird, prickly feeling she gets whenever she looks at the house. It's like a tickle from chilled bony fingers on her cheek, on her wrist, reaching through to the underside of her skin.

'I walked further into the hallway and heard this scratching sound on the floorboards.' He raked his blunt nails against the railings. Paint peeled off. 'It sounded like something was coming towards me. At which point, I really did run. I vaulted the gate like a hurdles pro. My mates never brought it up again and neither did I.'

'It was probably just a cat or something,' Tanya says.

'Yeah. A really big cat with overgrown claws.'

'Or something.'

'So now what?' Ram asks. 'Which window?'

Tanya points up to the top window. It's empty. Blank. The sash window looks like a hooded eye.

'Well, she's not up there,' Ram says. 'Case closed. Let's go.'

'Are you scared to go in?'

'Don't be ridiculous.' He opens the gate. It creaks wide. 'We could do with a scythe,' he says, trampling down the weeds in the garden.

'You mean April didn't have one in her Mary Poppins handbag?' Tanya says.

'Can we get on with this?' he says, checking his watch.

Tanya steps in front of him and knocks on the door. The knocker is in the shape of a rose and really does land with a 'thud'. She listens for scuttles or feet or anything at all. Nothing. No answer. Just the echo of the 'thud'. She shakes the padlocks on the heavy door. 'Don't suppose you know how to pick a lock?' she asks.

'You're the super brain. You figure it out.'

'Fine. I will. There must be another way in,' Tanya says. Brambles attach themselves to her clothes as she tries to get to the windows. They are all barred with iron and covered with ivy.

Ram moves away, picking his way through overgrown roses that have gone way beyond deadheading. He ducks down and under a bush, disappearing from sight.

'What're you doing?' she asks. She can hear him rustling in unseen undergrowth and swearing. LOTS of swearing. He reappears a few minutes later.

'There's a back gate at the side. It's pretty much covered with roses but we can climb over,' he says. *Now* he looks sweaty.

Ten minutes later, they're standing in the back garden, hoping that the dock leaves they're wiping over nettle rashes are not more nettles in disguise. Old trees rise over them and there's not one sliver of sun. In a day that could fry eggs on a belly button, it feels like they've never been warm.

'It must've been nice once. The garden,' Tanya says, wading through the grass, avoiding the huge hole where a badger has scurried up a pile of earth. 'It's huge.' She looks at a hedge growing out of a tub. It could've been elegant topiary. A squirrel, maybe. Now it looks like a woolly mammoth with its arse stuck in a bucket.

The stone house looks vulnerable from this view. Like when you're sitting behind one of your friends and see they've left the label in their shirt and it's not the size they say they are. Most of the windows at the back are broken, held together by webs. A conservatory leans against the house like a drunk friend at a party. Tiles have slipped from the roof and through the glass.

Something moves.

'Up there. Second floor,' Ram says, pointing up.

In the middle window of the middle storey, a girl places her palm against the window. Tanya can't see much of her face other than her jaw opening wide and closing around a word. HELP.

'Did you see that? She's mouthing to us to help her,' Tanya says, running to the conservatory and trying the door. It's bolted shut but the glass is broken in every frame.

'I'm not sure. She's definitely there, though,' Ram says, peering up, shielding his eyes against the bright sky.

'Give me the bag,' she yells to Ram. He hands it over. Emptying its contents out on the gravel, she wraps it around her hand and slams her fist into the cracked bottom pane.

'Whoah,' Ram says. 'What are you doing? Call the police. Now.'

'Like they're going to take me seriously,' Tanya says. She takes the glass out of the old dried putty, clearing the ground of any shards she finds.

Getting onto all fours, she begins to crawl through. On the other side, she stands up. It's like a scene from *Great Expectations*, if Miss Havisham were a keen gardener. Plant pots and jam jars and barrels of all sizes were lined up around the outsides of the conservatory. Each of them had a plant or flower growing inside and each of them was completely covered in spiderwebs.

These aren't just any old webs. They're as thick as football socks. She touches a strand and it clings to her, holding onto her fingers and dragging a marigold with it. Tanya brushes it away, hoping she hasn't shown how much it makes her skin creep.

A hammock is suspended in webs across one corner of the room, an ancient red velvet chaise longue lies at one end like a dried-out tongue; a table, wicker chairs around it as if waiting for three creepy bears, is laid out for afternoon tea. There are plates of desiccated scones and cake. A dead wasp lies in a jam tomb. Everything is covered with layers of dust, webs and shattered glass.

'Are you coming through?' she calls to Ram.

'Nope,' Ram replies.

Tanya tries the handle on the door into the house. It's locked. She tries to force it and, when that doesn't work, shoves the door with her shoulder. That doesn't work either. She takes a run at it. In films, people always bounce off the first time when they try this. Tanya doesn't exactly bounce. She hits the door with a whack and all the breath goes out of her.

'What *are* you doing?' Ram asks.

Not answering, she tries again. It's supposed to work on the second time, if not the third, but no. Her only reward is a slight cracking in the frame. The only other result is breathlessness and bruising. The fourth time, though, the cracking extends into a splintering that can be seen tearing through the wood. Plaster from above the door comes down like icing sugar.

A rushing wind blasts from inside the house. It sounds like it's crashing through rooms and breaking everything in its way. Upstairs, she hears a scream.

'We need to leave,' Ram shouts. 'Now.'

The wind builds into a crescendo, smashing through the windows, raining glass down through the glass roof. She crawls out, joining Ram and they run, covering their heads, to the gate. Tanya pulls herself up and swings over the top, grabbing onto the ivy to lower herself, but it tears away in her hands. She falls to the ground.

Ram drops down next to her. They're silent as they pick their way through the grabbing weeds of the front garden. When they're outside the front gate, they look up at the house. The girl stands again in the top window.

CHAPTER EIGHT

VIEW FROM THE ATTIC

I scrape at the webs on the window every day. They stick to my fingers but in time I make enough room to see outside. It's gone dark suddenly. Thunder echoes across rooftops that go on and on. The sky is the dark yellow-blue of a bruise on the underside of my arm. The rest of London hides behind the trees. I read about this city, watched TV programmes set here, loved the music made here and fought to reach it, but it doesn't even know I'm here. No one else knows, either.

I last heard from Baba four months ago on Whatsapp: I then lost my phone to the Mediterranean sea and by the time I got hold of another one and tried to call him his number wasn't recognised. He was ill, he said, that final time we talked. The crossing had been 'difficult' he said which, in Baba's language, means full of horror. He didn't want us to go through what he had, he said, but once a rocket hit our house, we had to leave Syria, just as he had.

It's been raining for hours. I hear it slam against the roof, upsetting the tiles. Last time I saw rain like this, I was in that small bedroom on my first night in London. It hit the window like tiny fists. In the room next door, another girl sobbed. Screamed for him to stop. The thunder did nothing to cover the sound.

I understand why people turn away from windows with girls in them. They look at our bodies and not our eyes. They don't want to know. It was the same all the way through our journey. From the moment we left Damascus, my status changed. The smuggler didn't look at us or ask our names as he bundled us into the car. My sister Yana and I were stuffed into the gap behind the front seats. Ummi lay on the back seat, covered, just as we were, with blankets and bags. I thought I could hardly breathe. In a few months I would find out what it was really like to not be able to breathe.

The screaming has started. It's happening again. I'm not in the same room but this house makes it play out time after time as if I were. The screaming next door turns to whimpering, her door slams. Slow footsteps to my door. Door key turns in the lock. The man who kidnapped me stands in the doorway, his hands on his hips.

My skin shrinks back to the bone.

I'm now trapped in a house filled with the journey's nightmares and I cannot hear a call for prayer. I have to imagine that sound and hope I get the times right. I often pray that, insha'Allah, in one of the windows behind the trees, my Baba is looking out, waiting for his lost family.

CHAPTER NINE

FACELESS ALICE

Ram appears on FaceTime. 'What do you want now?' he asks. He's in his room, which is as immaculate as ever. She angles the laptop so he can't see the piles of clothes growing on her bed. On her floor. Everywhere apart from the wardrobe. There are more important things to think about than tidiness. Her mum disagrees.

'So you believe me now, then?' Tanya says. She can't resist it.

Ram rolls his eyes.

'I've been looking into the house,' she says.

'Yeah? And what have you found?' he asks.

'Deeds on the house going back years,' she says, flicking through her notes. 'It was bought by a property developer last year. He's been given planning permission after a long wait and the property is due to be knocked down in a few weeks.'

'Who owned it before?'

'So you *are* interested then?'

'Get on with it, would you?'

'You know you said that people thought an old woman lived there?'

Ram nods. His eyes dart to the side then back.

'Is someone with you?' Tanya asks.

Ram looks to his left. 'April's here.'

April's head looms into view, close to the camera. 'Hello,' she says. Tanya can see right up her nostrils. April moves back and sits cross-legged next to Ram on his bed. 'Sounds like you've found us a haunted house.'

'I don't think we're going to find any ghosts,' Tanya says.

April looks disappointed.

'What about that old woman?' Ram says. 'Did she die there?'

'She did, in…' Tanya checks the screenshot of the death certificate. 'July last year. The developer bought it from her estate. Her name was Alice Parsons. She lived there for—'

'Did you say Alice?' Ram asks, moving closer to the screen.

'Yes, why?' she asks.

'I'll tell you in a minute. Carry on.'

'So she was there for years. She inherited it from her parents when they died, moved in and hardly ever went out. Everything was delivered to the door and left there. At some point overnight, the milk, bread, whatever, would be taken in and the rubbish put outside.'

'How do you know that?'

'I phoned some of her neighbours and said I was from the Mass Observation Centre at the local library. I had to sit through their stories as well.'

'And you've done all that since you got back?' April asks.

'Oh, I've done far more than that,' she says.

'Ram's found something, haven't you?' April nudges him.

'Alright,' he says, his eyes off the camera as he types. 'I'm getting to it. I'm sending you some links.' The links ping up. 'Go to the top one.'

Tanya clicks through to a site with a black background and grey text. 'It's pretty unreadable,' she says.

'I'm not sure they're trying to be inclusive,' Ram replies.

Tanya scans down the page. It's an urban legend site. People upload what they've heard from their best friend's third favourite hamster and then people add to it. The one Ram found is called 'Faceless Alice'. Now his excited face makes sense.

FACELESS ALICE,

SHOREDITCH, UK

I know you won't believe me but I swear this is true. Everything I'm about to tell was told to me by a close friend and I'd trust him with my life. In fact, he would go on to save my life, but that's a story for another time.

My friend Andy, about 21 at the time, was doing a teacher training placement at a school in Shoreditch. He was walking home one day when he looked up at this old stone house, complete mess it was, he said, and saw a girl in the top left window. He said she was banging at the window but he couldn't hear anything. He couldn't see her face but thought she must be too far away. The next day he went back with a friend. They broke into the house and looked around. There were weird markings on the floor, he said, and they were about to leave when they saw her. She sort of floated down the stairs. Andy thought she must have been 13, 14 but couldn't be sure because she didn't have any eyes, mouth, nose, ears, forehead. Her face was a blank oval, completely smooth as if her features had been wiped away.

She reached out to them, a strange strangled noise coming from her throat. Andy was nearest the door and started to run and thought his friend was just behind. When Andy looked back, the girl with no face was sifting through a pile of dust and his friend was nowhere to be seen. It was only when he looked down that he saw his friend's glasses and cufflinks in the dust.

There were links to similar stories about the house, the faceless girl's malevolence growing each time. The more recent the story, the more it had grown. The last one was the most chilling.

FACELESS ALICE,

SHOREDITCH, UK

I don't want to say much. I suppose I feel sorry for her, all alone in that house. That house contains evil that I've only seen in dreams. Faceless Alice is not the worst of it. She heralds something far worse. I know this isn't the place to say this, but if you get out, you'd think you'd be one of the lucky ones. But you're not. The loneliness doesn't go away afterwards. The house infects you. This site is for people who love this kind of thing but it should be a warning to the curious, only come if you can handle your own nightmares. They're waiting for you.

* * *

There's a grainy picture at the bottom. The photo was maybe thirty, forty years old, the house in a much better state, but it was instantly recognisable as the stone house.

'I've zoomed in,' Ram says, leaning forward. 'The same girl is at the top front window.'

'It can't be the same girl,' Tanya says.

Another message pings in. Tanya clicks on the image. He's sent the blown-up image. It's really poor quality, but then photos were at that time. If you didn't know better, you'd think everyone in the '70s had sideburns, sprinklers and smudges for faces.

'All I can see,' she says, 'is that there's a person in a dress standing close to the window. You can't tell if it's the same girl.'

'That's because it's Faceless Alice! She hasn't got a face, it's kind of her brand,' Ram says, coming near to the screen. 'She haunts the house, appears to her chosen victims and turns them to dust.'

'I think someone's getting carried away,' Tanya says in a sing-song voice. 'We saw her screaming, remember? Hard to scream without a face.'

Ram's forehead furrows. 'Don't remember that part. Do you really think it's a coincidence that a girl appears at the same window of the same house?'

'I don't know *what* it is yet. You seem to *want* her to be a ghost or something.'

'What else could she be? The same story coming up over decades and *we* saw the same thing this afternoon. And the owner was called Alice! It all fits. Look I'm trying to help here. What more do you want from me?'

'She appreciates it, don't you, Tanya?' April says.

'Of course I do,' Tanya replies. 'It's great you're taking an interest.' She manages to stop herself saying 'for once' out loud. 'So how do you think Alice Parsons could appear at the window, looking the same for forty years?'

'Don't know,' says Ram. 'That's the mystery, isn't it?'

'Tanya Adeola, would you get down here *now*,' Vivian shouts up the stairs.

'Time to go,' Ram says.

Tanya nods. April waves goodbye then disappears.

'Now, young lady,' Vivian says. She's got the 'young lady' out. Must be serious.

Tanya closes her laptop and swings her legs off the bed. She walks around the piles of clothes and opens the door. 'What is it?' she says, peering down into the hall.

Vivian presses her forefinger between her eyebrows. One of her migraines must be circling. 'I've been calling you down for dinner for the last ten minutes.'

'Sorry, Mum, didn't hear you.' Her mum raises an eyebrow. 'Really, I didn't.'

'What are you doing up there that's so distracting?' Vivian folds her arms.

'Research,' Tanya says.

'For your homework?'

'I'm working on it at home, yes.'

Vivian sighs. 'Dinner's ready. That's all I've been trying to say.' She closes her eyes. 'It's on the table. Going cold. It's already late due to you running about the place.'

Tanya feels the familiar mix of anger and sympathy towards her mum. They're like competing ivy. She goes through to the kitchen and sits down. The strands of ivy writhe. It always happens. It's why silence is so brilliant.

'So,' Vivian says, spooning out lasagna. 'What are you working on?'

Silence obviously isn't an option. Fantastic. 'We're looking at local history,' Tanya says. 'Houses in particular.' Thinking on her feet or rather on the kitchen chair is an established art in the Adeola household. 'I wondered if you could help.'

Vivian softened. 'What are you looking at?'

'Do you know an old house, the only one of a row of big detached places that wasn't sold off for developments? It used to belong to an old woman called Alice Parsons.'

'I'd forgotten about the Parsons' house,' Vivian says. She shivers lightly.

Tanya takes a bite of lasagna with salad. She hadn't realised how hungry she was.

'You're not to go there,' Vivian says, her face hardening again. 'Absolutely not. I'm going to see your teacher tomorrow and ask what she's doing getting you to look into terrible places like that.' Her hand clamps against her forehead.

'It was nothing to do with Miss Quill. I chose it. It's my fault.'

Vivian humphs. 'Now I can believe *that*,' she says.

'Why shouldn't I go there?' Tanya asks.

'Take my word for it,' Vivian says. 'No good can come from an old stone house.'

CHAPTER TEN

GREASY SPOON

'Two things make this planet passable,' Miss Quill says, reaching across for a mug as the café owner brings their order to the table. 'Coffee is one of them.'

'What's the other one?' Tanya asks.

'If *you* don't know then I feel more sorry for you than I do normally. Besides, some things should be kept secret.' She takes a huge slurp of coffee. A smile threatens her lips, then skulks away.

'Thanks for meeting us, Miss Quill,' Tanya says.

Miss Quill looks at her breakfast. 'A "greasy spoon" you call it? Why stop at that utensil? It could be a greasy knife, cup or kitchen clock, pick anything you see, it's greasy – if you *can* see it beneath the layers of spattered fat.' She looks over at the owner behind the counter. 'Another sausage.

47

Thank you.' She slices into her egg with the precision and enthusiasm of someone used to wielding knives.

'We'd like your help,' Tanya says. 'Well, *I* would. Ram and April are here because I bribed them with waffles.'

Ram raises a fork filled with waffle, bacon and maple syrup. 'And I'll be out of here as soon as I've finished this.'

'You'd better hurry up, then, Miss Adeola,' Miss Quill says. She lifts phlegmy goop off the top of an egg and wrinkles her nose.

Tanya tells Miss Quill about what happened at the stone house and the research they'd done. Behind them, more sausage spits in the pan. 'The others didn't believe me. I'm still not sure that they do.'

'It's not that we don't believe you,' April says.

'It's just that we don't care,' Ram says.

'You were *there*,' Tanya says, turning on Ram. 'You saw it.'

Ram shrugs and eats more waffle.

'So what do you think, Miss Quill?' Tanya asks.

Miss Quill picks the bacon rind up from the plate and sucks on it. 'I think it's none of your business. And it's certainly none of mine. Don't you think we're dealing with enough shadows as it is, without adding ones that *aren't* a threat to us?' She places her knife and fork in a cross formation.

'That's not how they do things here, Miss Quill,' April says.

'Yeah,' says Ram. 'You don't need to ward off the plate vampires.'

'Do you think I don't know that?' Miss Quill says. She quickly changes the knife and fork to the usual standing shoulder-to-shoulder, feet at the bottom of the plate, position. Tanya gets the briefest of glances into a world where crossed cutlery is standard.

'Can *you* help, though, Miss Quill?' Tanya says.

'Absolutely not. *And you* should concentrate on your work,' Miss Quill says. 'Ghost stories are best when it's cold outside. It is *far* from cold outside. You would be better off looking into whether the Rift is causing an uplift in temperatures.'

'If we wait for things to attack us, we're always on the defensive,' Tanya says. 'If something odd is going on near the Rift, don't you think it's our duty to investigate it?'

'Duty?' Miss Quill says, taking a piece of toast from the pile and buttering it in angry strokes. 'I have enough duty looking after Charlie.'

'If we only look after ourselves, if we only respond when *we* are under attack, and not when someone else is, then we can't really expect anyone to help *us*,' April says.

Miss Quill's teeth crunch into the toast. She chews slowly, looking at Tanya through narrowed eyes.

'If Tanya's wrong, then we can all laugh at her,' Ram says.

Tanya glares at him.

'That's the best argument I've heard all day,' Miss Quill says.

'So you'll help?'

'Only if you agree to stop if I say there's nothing further to look at.' She points at Tanya. 'Which I am anticipating to be the case.'

'Agreed. So,' Tanya says, leaning forward. She gets bean juice on her sleeve. 'Are we talking ghosts? Poltergeists? Aliens?'

'Well,' Miss Quill says with a sigh. 'I suppose we'd better find out, hadn't we?'

CHAPTER ELEVEN

THE CROSSING

We got out over the mountains. It wasn't far over the border, but we had to keep stopping to hide from planes. Yana was so tired that Ummi and me took turns carrying her until our backs and legs couldn't take it. On the other side, in Kahramanmaras, we were taken to our first camp. Ummi had her ID and some money but we had to leave everything else. She cried when we were given a small tent for just the three of us, and the day's rations.

Between the street of shops and the temporary school, the radio playing my favourite songs, enough water to wash for prayer, and the family in the tent next door who gave us blankets and a small table, it would be the most welcoming and equipped of the camps we stayed in, but it was still a town of three thousand tents during the end of winter. The nights were bad. It was when people cried the most. Ummi told us to always stay together and look out for each other. She gave us some of her rations and joked that her limbs were becoming like those of an olive tree. She stayed up at nights, watching. We didn't know why, then.

One night, Ummi suggested that we should stay there, wait until we heard if Baba was safe and had reached London. But Yana and I said no. We wanted Baba. And so Ummi paid almost all of our money to someone who said he could get us from Turkey to Greece. He promised that it would be safe. I no longer trust promises.

He put us on a plastic dinghy with 120 other people. The sea spat salt at us, drying our faces and hands. It tipped backwards and forwards. Yana clung to my leg and looked at me with huge eyes.

I held onto one of the handles, guarding it from anyone else who wanted it. Ummi kept saying that it would be good, that we would see Baba soon. I don't know whether we hit a big wave, or if something went wrong with the steering, but the dinghy tipped. Our side dipped towards the sea. I held on with both hands. The water surged in, taking my plastic bag with my new phone inside. I could hear Ummi shouting for us to 'hold on'. Seeing Yana headed for the water, I swept her up and circled her with my arms, gripping the handle and pushing back so that I didn't crush her. People were screaming, falling into the sea. I was kicked in the face, my headscarf pulled at by someone in the water but I didn't try and help them. That's what I remember most. Thinking I couldn't help. No, not couldn't. Wouldn't.

It seemed hours but was probably minutes. The dinghy stabilised and I was still holding on. Yana's head rested on the side of the dinghy. I picked her up and she murmured, eyes closed. I looked round. Ummi wasn't there. I called out for her but I couldn't hear my voice among the many.

CHAPTER TWELVE

STRANGER ON THE INSIDE

It's dusk by the time Tanya arrives at the house. She's the first one here. Maybe none of them is going to turn up, maybe they all only reluctantly agreed so they could think of her standing alone here and laugh. She slips on her big jumper and leans against the railings. She'll give them ten minutes, then leave.

Quick footsteps approach behind her. Tanya turns and sees April hurrying towards her. 'I passed Matteusz and Charlie on the way,' April says. And there they are, walking slowly towards the house.

Miss Quill turns up next, followed five minutes later by Ram. They stand in its shadow, looking up. The London gulls are silent and no one's talking. It's weird. Normally *someone* is saying too much, usually her, but not

55

even Miss Quill has any terse words. She's looking up at the house with her head on one side. It's like the house infects everything around it. The streaks of grey clouds against purple make it look as if the sky is peeling back to stone.

'This is a bad idea,' Ram says. 'We shouldn't go in there.' April links her hand with his. 'At least not for very long.'

'Let's not stand around staring, someone will send for the police,' Miss Quill says, walking through the gate and kicking back weeds as if she owned the place.

'Did you hear back from the police?' Charlie asks. He's stroking Matteusz's back as he walks behind him but it's not clear who he's reassuring most, him or Matteusz. Both, probably. Ram and April stand close together. Tanya pulls her jumper round tighter. Everyone's got someone. Apart from Miss Quill, and who knows if she lost someone or left someone behind?

'They said they broke in – look, you can see,' Tanya says, pointing to the door where it has been forced off its hinges, wood splintering where it looks as if a heavy weight has been heaved at the lock. 'The officer said he couldn't see any sign of someone being detained, only of rough sleeping. It was empty, though.'

Miss Quill makes a noise somewhere between a humph and a snort. 'As if they'd be able to see if anything was going on.' She looks round the garden, tutting. 'You can't move for dandelions. Horrible things. Not as bad as buttercups, though. Never let someone put one under your chin to see if you like butter.'

'Why?' Ram asks. 'Are they really doing something else? Are buttercups really alien spy devices, gathering information for an invasion?'

'No,' Miss Quill replies, peering in upturned plant pots. 'Asking about butter is courting disguised as coy nonsense. If they can't ask you a direct question then they're not worth talking to.'

'The officer did seem a bit freaked out on the phone,' Tanya says.

'Maybe he doesn't like phones,' Charlie says. 'I don't.'

'You didn't have a problem using yours earlier today,' Matteusz says, grinning. He waves his phone at Charlie.

'That's enough of that,' Miss Quill says, shoving open the door that the police had kindly broken open for them.

They walk through into what must once have been a grand hallway. Thin slices of light shine through the sides of heavy curtains, showing up a high ceiling and a wooden staircase sweeping up to the first floor. An ornate railing runs across the open first-floor landing. There's a funny smell. Dust, old shoe soles and mould.

Miss Quill yanks back the curtains. One of them comes away from the rail, crumpling to the floor. A floorboard creaks as if in protest.

'Shouldn't we leave it as it is?' Tanya asks. 'Just look around?'

'I need to see what I'm doing, thank you, Miss Adeola. If something *is* here then I do not want to be surprised. Here,' Miss Quill says, reaching into her bag and taking out six torches. She turns her one on and hands the others around.

'See,' says April, nudging Ram. 'It's not just me.'

'Oh, great,' Ram says. 'I'm dating Miss Quill Mark 2.'

'That's an insult,' Miss Quill says, over her shoulder.

'To you or me?' April says.

'To Miss Quill Mark 2,' Miss Quill Mark 1 says. 'She did her best but war was not for her.'

Charlie shakes his head, closes his eyes and mutters something in another language that sounds a bit like prayer. Sometimes it's best not to ask.

Tanya shines her torch around the hallway. Sleeping bags slump in one corner, surrounded by empty cans and packets of crisps. Cobwebs cover everything apart from the floor and the banister of the staircase. Little piles of dust are dotted around, as if someone's been sweeping and forgotten to clear up. Miss Quill takes samples of the dust and the thick cobwebs.

They walk through into a small room with an armchair, a fireplace and loads and loads of dolls in different national costumes. An aunt gave Tanya one of them once. She'd brought it back from a holiday in Spain, which felt very much like, 'I get to go on holiday, you get to have a weird flamenco doll with no genitals and castanets stuck to her palms.'

The blank-eyed plastic girls stare out from their shelves in crisp national dress. There's a lot of man-made fabric in the room. One hot day and they'll all catch fire.

'Given how weird this place is, how about we all split up and go explore? Like in a horror film,' Ram says, 'that way we can get killed off in turn until one of us is left.'

'That'll be me, then,' April says.

'You'll be the first to go,' Tanya says. 'I'll be last, having worked out that it was Charlie all along.'

'Why me?'

'It's always the gorgeous one.'

'Then it should be me, obviously,' Ram says.

'Are you really arguing about which one of you is the serial killer while we're walking round a spooky old house?' Tanya asks.

'Would you please all SHUT UP,' April shouts, whirling around with the torch, then takes a step back as if she's surprised even herself.

'Thank you, April,' Miss Quill calls out, already walking through into the adjoining room. 'You saved me the trouble.'

Torchlight criss-crosses the room. It's a kitchen with all the usual kitchen things in it but about a hundred years old. Free-standing oven. Battered fridge freezer, empty. A sink old-style wide that plates would smash in if they slipped, next to it a draining board with a saucepan, bowl, plate and mug in it. They were still wet. 'Someone *has* been here,' Tanya says. 'Only one, I think, and recently.' She puts down her bag and looks around, opening cupboards.

'Probably one of the homeless people the policeman mentioned,' April says.

'Could be the girl we saw in the window,' Tanya replies.

'Come on, why would someone trapped inside and screaming for help do the washing up?' Ram asks. His tone is scathing.

'I don't know. Maybe she's forced to?' Tanya says, anger rising. A strong picture of the young woman came into her head, of her being shouted at and flinching, dodging back from an open fist.

'Stop squabbling and be quiet,' Miss Quill hisses. 'I agreed to come along on this foolish quest of yours, Tanya, if you'd do as I say. If you don't do as I say then I'll make *you* do the washing up in the staff room for the rest of the term. Teachers get through a lot of food. There are so many jam doughnuts in there they look like vampires at lunch time.' She pauses. 'That would, in fact, explain a lot.'

'The oven is still hot,' April says, placing her hand against it. 'The gas must still be connected.' She walks across to the tap. 'And the water's still on.' She tries the light switch. Nothing happens. 'But not the electricity. Why would the gas and water be connected if no one's living here?'

'Maybe the developers keep it on?' Tanya says. 'They'll need water. Don't know why they'd need gas but not electricity though.'

'You two are actually enjoying this, aren't you?' Ram says, shaking his head. He picks one of the empty tin cans out of the bin between his thumb and forefinger. 'Whoever it is *really* likes tomato soup. Must be twenty tins of the stuff in there. Urgh.' He washes his hand under the tap and flicks water at April.

'Tinned pasta, too. And beans. And mandarin segments,' Tanya says, pointing to a cupboard stacked with the stuff.

'Orange, slippery and tinned,' Ram says. 'That's a balanced diet.'

'Can we get on?' Miss Quill says. She sounds bored. 'We are not undertaking an inventory.'

'Is anyone here?' Tanya shouts out. 'We're here to help.'

'Were you listening when I told you to be quiet, Tanya? Or did you just think you'd ignore me, given that I said I'd join if, and only if, you followed my lead?' Miss Quill places her hands on her hips and stares. She doesn't blink. She could be a staring champion.

'I'm sorry but we're here to find her,' Tanya says. 'It's no good if she doesn't know we're here.'

'That doesn't mean announcing yourself like a teen town crier,' Miss Quill says.

'Yes, Miss Quill,' Tanya says, opening a door into a utility room. An old washing machine squats in the corner. Its one big eye gleams in the torch beam like a Cyclops. Pieces of rope hang from left to right across the ceiling. Two T-shirts and a huge jumper are draped across them, just about dry, although the material has a slightly damp feel.

'Well, *someone's* definitely here,' Miss Quill says. Ram knocks a tin off the shelf in his hurry to get into the utility room. It rolls across the floor. 'And I think it's likely that she, or someone, now knows we're here.'

She places a finger on her lips. They listen for noises.
Nothing.

Miss Quill unlocks the door into the conservatory. 'This is where you came in?' she asks, looking at the draped furniture and the apples that had scattered across the tiled floor.

'Waste not, want not,' April says, picking up a bruised apple and eating it. 'Urgh.' She makes a face and looks at the fruit. It's brown and woolly inside. The other apples have turned rotten as well, wrinkling up as if they've been on a sunbed too long.

'Those apples you gave us didn't last long, April,' Tanya says.

'I had one of them from the same pack today,' April says, frowning. 'It was fine.'

'Come on,' Miss Quill says, 'there's the rest of the house to not find anyone in. Sooner we finish, the sooner I can get back to *Orange is the New Black*.'

They walk back into the reception hall and then a small dining room on the other side. A tall shape stands in the corner. Miss Quill shoots her arm out, blocking their way. Tanya flashes her torch at it. It's a standard lamp. Ram laughs, then covers his mouth. The shadow of the shade on the wall looks like a detective in a fedora.

A long table takes up the centre of the room. It's covered in comics, all laid out in double-spreads. Most are yellow and brittle. Miss Quill picks one up. One of the pages falls to the floor.

'Careful,' says Ram, 'they could be valuable.'

Miss Quill places it back down and scans the table full of old *Beano*s and *Dandy*s. 'You're sure there were no kids here?'

'We didn't find any evidence when we looked into Alice's history,' Tanya says, walking around the room. 'No birth or death certificates, no school attendance or anything else.' There's another stack of newspapers at the end of the table, all copies of the same paper, from June last year. Miss Quill takes one and puts it in her bag. As Tanya crouches down to read one, she notices six piles of dust at equal distance around the table, as if guests at a last supper were blasted to ashes in their chairs. Some host, this old lady.

They move through to the hallway, aware of their footsteps echoing around the house, and into the lounge. Miss Quill opens the velvet curtains but hardly any light comes in. The sun has ducked out of sight. They're completely reliant on torches now.

A huge box of an ancient television is in the corner, topped with dusty glasses and a decanter of something now evaporated. Miss Quill sniffs at the lip of the decanter. 'Amontillado,' she says.

Two armchairs are placed either side of a fire. Grey ash covers the grate. April sits down. Dust rises, making her cough. 'If there *are* ghosts in the house,' she says, looking around the room, 'then they're really quiet, well-behaved ones.'

'The kind of ghosts you can take home to your mum,' Ram replies.

Tanya says nothing, embarrassment growing. Looks like she's brought everyone here for nothing. Perhaps she imagined the girl. Maybe Ram is going along with it to set her up. Any minute now he'll turn round and laugh at her.

Ram lifts the lid off a ginger jar on the mantelpiece. 'Are you in there, Faceless Alice?' he says, in a seance-spooky voice. 'Speak to us.' Not the actions of a boy who wants to placate.

'If there *is* nothing here,' April says, 'and that looks likely, then we're trespassing for no reason.'

'Bet we saw one of the homeless people,' Ram says. Tanya knows he's speaking to her but doesn't meet his gaze. 'She probably ran when the police came.'

'Or when you and Tanya paid a visit,' Miss Quill says. 'I'd run away from you two if I had the chance. From all of you.' She looks around the room. 'Where's Charlie? And Matteusz?'

'Haven't seen them,' Tanya says.

Miss Quill mutters to herself and strides out of the lounge into the hallway and stops so abruptly at the entrance to the dining room that Tanya bumps into her.

Charlie and Matteusz are snogging. Charlie is sitting on the dining-room table with Matteusz standing between his knees. Charlie wraps his legs around Matteusz's and draws him nearer.

Miss Quill opens her mouth to speak but Tanya digs her in the ribs. She shakes her head. If Charlie and Matteusz notice them, they either don't show it or don't care. Tanya and Miss Quill move back into the hall.

'Well, isn't this a fun way to spend an evening?' Miss Quill says.

'I'm sorry,' Tanya says.

'I would say it's not your fault, but...'

A crash comes from the next floor. Charlie and Matteusz run out, meeting the rest of them in the hallway. 'Stay there, all of you,' Miss Quill says, sprinting up the stairs.

None of them stays there.

CHAPTER THIRTEEN

DON'T LOOK

I was on the first floor when they came in. I crouched, staying close to the railings. Their torches didn't find me. They're so busy looking that they can't see.

Now they're running up the stairs, led here by the house. What's it doing? What does it want?

This is a game to them. If they've come to search out horrors, they will find them. Only not the ones they think. They'll find their own nightmares staring and asking questions they'd buried. At this moment, Ummi sits next to me. She's lost her headscarf and her hair is wet. She refuses to look at me. If I speak to her, she turns her head away. I've said I'm sorry, again and again.

The girl who saw me is the only one here to help, the others don't believe. If she does, and I can get out of the house, I won't see my mother's drowned face any more but then I also won't see her happy face, the one I catch a glimpse of in corridors.

I crawl under the bed so that I'm doubly hidden. Part of me wills her to find me, another part wants her to go away and never come back, for her sake and mine.

CHAPTER FOURTEEN

LEAVE NOW

Miss Quill stops on the first floor. 'One time,' she says when they all reach the landing, 'you'll do exactly what I say.' She's not even slightly out of breath. She looks round, calculating. Several doors lead off the landing. Another set of stairs leads up to the next floor.

Tanya can hear her own breathing. Is it normally that loud? And her heart. If she can just stop it thumping so loudly then maybe no one else will know how scared she is.

A second crash comes from above them. Miss Quill is off up the next set of stairs to the top floor. The ceilings are lower up here and the corridors tighter. It feels as if the walls are pressing in.

The loudest crash yet.

'It's in the end room,' Miss Quill whispers.

Charlie swallows, his Adam's apple bobbing as if in a Halloween barrel.

Miss Quill gestures for them to walk behind her down the corridor. The carpet is old and worn, its pattern swirling like vortices in the torchlight.

'No, please,' a woman's voice pleads behind the door. Miss Quill tries to open the door but it's locked. She takes out her skeleton key and raises an eyebrow at us. The door clicks open.

It's a large room with a low ceiling, slanted on the side that looks out over the garden. A sliver of moon picks out a wooden chest of drawers, fallen onto its front. Its drawers are scattered and shattered across the room.

Their torches flash onto two made-up beds, a trunk and a wardrobe. Tanya gets down on her hands and knees by the beds. She lifts up the drapes that hang over the first one. Her heart is too loud again. If someone's under there, they'll hear it. The torchlight shines right through to the other side. Under the bedstead lies one of the national costume dolls. She wears a gold headdress.

Something scuttles above them. Plaster flakes from the ceiling.

'There's an attic,' April whispers, pointing to a hatch. 'Whoever it is must have gone up there just before we came in.'

'But how? There's no ladder in here,' Ram says. He checks in the wardrobe to make sure. It's full of musty-smelling dresses. A moth flies out, heading for his torch.

'It's probably up there and can be pulled down when you need it,' April says.

Charlie hauls the chest of drawers upright and drags it across the floor, placing it underneath the hatch. Using Matteusz for support, he steps up and pushes at the board. 'It won't move,' he says.

The scuttling pauses, then moves quickly across the floorboards.

'It's going this way,' April says, following the sound. She walks out of the door into the hallway.

It slams shut.

'April!' Ram shouts, pulling at the handle. It doesn't move. Charlie joins in but it's not going anywhere.

'I can't get in,' April shouts through the door.

Miss Quill uses the key again but it's fixed in place. Something is stopping it turn.

'We can't get out,' Ram shouts.

'Something is holding it on the other side,' Matteusz says.

'It's not me,' April shouts, then suddenly screams. There's a thud, then a dragging sound.

'April. APRIL!' Ram shouts.

No answer.

He crashes into the door with his shoulder. 'It won't move.'

'We'd better hope someone is on the other side,' Tanya replies. 'Otherwise...'

'Don't say it,' Charlie interrupts.

'Why?'

'Leave it, Tanya,' Miss Quill says.

Tanya leaves it.

'So now I'm trapped in a room with you lot,' Ram says. 'Great. Thanks, Tanya.'

'So now I'm blamed when something *does* happen as well as when it doesn't?'

'We shouldn't have been here in the first place,' Charlie says.

'You were the one who said that it's our duty to check out abnormalities,' Tanya says. 'And looks like I was right to be worried.'

'This isn't the time for "I told you so",' Miss Quill says. Her ear is close to the wall, as if listening to it.

A screeching sound comes from down the landing. The door opens, slowly, as if it had never been locked. Closes after them.

They run into the hallway, torches held out. Ram pushes past until he gets to the top of the staircase. April lies at the top. Not moving.

'Don't touch her,' Miss Quill says. 'She could be injured.' She checks her pulse, listens to her chest and opens her eyelid.

'Is she okay?' Ram asks. His voice breaks in the middle.

'She's been knocked out but she's breathing.'

The wind careers down the hall, knocking pictures off the wall.

April murmurs and tries to move her head. She winces.

'Don't move too quickly,' Miss Quill says. 'You may have concussion.' She looks up. 'Someone phone for an ambulance.'

Ram crouches next to April and holds her hand while Matteusz takes out his phone and, moving closer to the stairs, calls 999. Charlie looks over to him, worry sharp on his face. It's as if they are linked. Tanya can't imagine being linked like that. She'd like to. Longs to. It's like the front of her chest is pulling her towards someone but she doesn't know who or how they'll be found. It's always there, that longing, for someone who'd know her properly, not as the smart arse in the wrong year, the girl with the answer to everything, but as the girl who doesn't know what to do.

Someone who wants to be next to her. Someone to learn with, and not just the prame numbers of the Renyalin series.

And then it starts.

The howling.

It's in the room they've just come from, sounding like a wounded animal slamming against the walls of a cage. Flashes come from under the door.

Thunder claps.

A tempest trapped in an attic room.

'Move,' Miss Quill shouts, running back, gathering up April till she's just about on her feet. 'Storms never stay in one place.' She looks over her shoulder with pain on her face, then starts down the stairs, April held close to her. Ram and Matteusz follow.

With a crash, the door flies open. It hurtles towards Tanya and she ducks, twisting her neck to watch it flip over the banister and down to the ground floor. Rain pours from clouds inside the house.

'I said MOVE!' Miss Quill shouts. They move.

At the bottom of the first set of stairs, something stands in their way. Some*one* stands in their way. A girl. Black hair in a bob that stops at her chin, framing what would be her face.

If she had a face.

The front of her head is curved and completely smooth.

No eyes.

No nose.

No m–

Wait.

A mouth appears in the egg-like face. It opens. Baby teeth fall out, adult jaws open wide. Screaming comes from lungs far bigger than her thin body can carry.

Her hands reach out. She walks towards Ram, the wind blowing her hair around her like a dark halo.

He runs down the second set of stairs. Tanya slips round the girl and grabs onto Ram's shirt, keeping close, feeling Charlie hold onto her shoulder. She stops at the bottom, chest heaving.

'Tanya,' Miss Quill calls out from some way back. Her voice is steady, slow. A warning.

Tanya turns round.

Her mum is slumped on the floor, her shoulders heaving with silent sobs. She holds her chest as if her heart might fall out. Vivian sees Tanya and her face changes into a snarl. 'Don't you come near me,' she says, getting to her feet.

'Mum?' Tanya says.

'You never gave him a moment's peace. Did you think he wanted a kid? Really? He did a great job at pretending, I'll give him that.'

'It wasn't my fault,' Tanya says, faltering.

'"It wasn't my fault",' Vivian sneers. 'Pathetic. You take away my love and look what I'm left with. You!'

Tanya reaches for her. 'Mum, please.'

Vivian holds her hands up and shakes her head. 'I can't even look at you, let alone touch you,' she says and walks towards the stairs. She fades before she gets to the first step.

Charlie puts one arm round Tanya. It's an awkward hug. 'That never happened, did it?' he asks.

'No,' she says. 'I've thought it, though.'

'It wasn't real,' he says.

'Then what was it?' Tanya asks. She can't see for tears and rain. 'What is this place?'

April moans. 'I don't feel good,' she says. She sways.

Miss Quill picks her up. Ram stands on one side of her, Matteusz the other. Matteusz takes Tanya's arm. His eyes are closed. On all sides of them, war begins. Men march with guns. Smoke rises from piles of bones. The crying of rockets. The echo of gunfire. Tents on fire. Agony. Injury. Laughing men and slamming doors.

As they make their way through the haze, she feels something push past her. She turns but can't even see her hand held out in front of her.

All that can be heard is a web of voices, all caught up in each other:

'You left us here. You left us for dead. Some of us are still here, Charlie.'

'You'll never be best. How could you be? Look at you.'

'I loved you, Andrea. I'll never forgive you.'

It's not even clear if they are voices, feelings or ghosts. They're as hard to grasp as the smoke cloaking the house.

The lights of the ambulance flash through the sides of the curtains. 'Get out,' Miss Quill says. 'All of you.'

Tanya goes towards the door then stops. 'My bag,' she says, realising it's no longer across her chest.

'Leave it,' Miss Quill shouts, pushing her towards the door.

Tanya twists round and runs back, through the doll room into the kitchen. The bag is on the table. On the counter, where it had been covered in dust, words had been spelled out in alphabet spaghetti:

LEAVE NOW.

CHAPTER FIFTEEN

THE HOUSE IS ANGRY

Doors slam open. Doors slam shut.

I soothe the house, stroke its walls and tell it that the police and visitors meant no harm. They're trying to help. It should let me talk to them, not lock me away. It's keeping me in the attic room as punishment for leaving her a message.

I didn't dare come out and meet her. I thought she might find me, hoped she would, but then the house made something else happen. It always does. I followed them down the stairs, trying not to take in any of the horror around me. I whispered as I passed her on the stairs. She didn't see me. Too much chaos. I don't even know if she heard me.

I don't like being stuck in a room. The house must know this: it sees one of my nightmares walking with heavy boots across its floorboards. Maybe that's why it conjures them. It wants me to see them. It must hate me for being here, but then why keep me at all? Why lock all the doors when I try and leave?

At least this time the windows are not painted shut. The webs cover them but I can stick my nose through a hole in the glass to breathe air that does not smell of dust and mould. In that cupboard bedroom, all I had was the corner of a window where I scratched away the whitewash and peered through, down to the street. London carried on as if nothing was happening.

Here though, I have trees outside and a squirrel that I've called Yana. Yana twists her head to look at me sometimes. Twitches her nose. The woman with the orange hair reminded me of Yana, both squirrel Yana and my sister. Bright, curious, open. It is difficult to think of my sister but someone should. There is no one else left to remember her, to remember any of them. I see her in the house, sometimes. Those are the good days. A few days ago I was in the kitchen making soup, when I heard her laugh. I ran into the room of dolls and there she was, on the floor, her legs stuck out. She held a Spanish doll in one hand, an Iranian one in the other and they were dancing to music I couldn't hear.

'Yana,' I said. She looked up at me, smiled, and disappeared. That was the longest I've seen her in a very long time. Most days, I am lucky to catch a glimpse of her sleeve as she runs down the corridor, or smell the fresh lemon drink she loved.

I wish she were in the attic with me all the time. We could play together. I could read to her from this trunk of books. There are 108 books in the trunk. I've counted them ten times. They're a bit young for me but they would be perfect for her. I was teaching her how to read English before. Even when war was everywhere, we'd sit and read. These books are perfect for me, though, in a way. Stories of horses, ballet shoes, skating shows, an American girl eating apples in attics, boarding schools and safe adventures with a yellow dog. It's as if they open a door into a world where hardship is a school bully or losing just one or two of your family members. It feels safe. Comforting. And I haven't felt safe or comforted in a very long time. I get lost in that world until the house is so cold that I cannot turn the pages any more.

The house is beginning to calm. Its rages, like thunder, are further apart. It shakes only slightly now. I curl up under the blanket on the bed near the window. At least she came back, that girl. The one from the window. And now I know her name. One of her friends called her it and she has so many friends. Her name is Tanya.

CHAPTER SIXTEEN

MEMORY BOX

Miss Quill waits until Charlie has gone to bed and for quiet to take hold of her house. She then takes out the bracelet from the small box. It is so light it seems to be non-existent. It is made of an element that carries little mass yet can hold the memories of those it's bonded with.

It is the red of dried blood. She doesn't have any photographs that she can look back on, this is all she has. Holding onto the bracelet, she closes her eyes. Snapchats of memories appear and disappear. She's looked at this so many times but has never shared it with someone else, so how come she saw what she saw in the corridor of the stone house? Who has harvested these memories? And why?

Miss Quill places the bracelet back in the box and locks it in her bedside cabinet. Nothing good can come of this.

CHAPTER SEVENTEEN

DREAMWEAVING

Tanya wakes up, sweating through the thin sheet. She grabs hold of the side of the bed and turns on the light. She looks around. She's in her bedroom, in her house. Her bedroom is a mess. Clothes have been flung everywhere, books lie in toppled towers on the carpet. It's exactly as she left it. She dreamed that she was back at the stone house and her mum was trying to turn her to dust, to send her to her dad, she said.

Shuffles down the corridor outside. The door opens.

Vivian stands blinking in the doorway. 'What's happened?' she says through a wide yawn. 'You were screaming.'

'Bad dream,' Tanya says.

'About your dad, like before?' Vivian says, coming over to sit on the edge of the bed.

'Kind of,' Tanya says. She used to have bad dreams where her dad appeared, now Vivian showed up. She won't tell Vivian about the development, it'd upset her too much and when Vivian is upset, the whole house comes to a painful stop.

'I would give anything to dream about him more often,' Vivian says. 'Good dreams, though, not the ones you are having. I don't want that for you, Tanya.'

'It's complicated,' Tanya says. Dreams about her dad used to start sweet and crisp and turn as bad as the spilled apples in the conservatory. She's shivering.

'Yes,' Vivian says, patting the bed so that she doesn't sit on any part of Tanya. She shifts closer to her daughter. 'How could it be different? Your father left us too soon and we are left with memories. It's hard to make sense of it.' She takes Tanya's hand and squeezes it. 'I know he misses you. I know he is there now, watching over me as I try and bring you up without him.'

Tanya pulls her hand away. 'Do you really think that's helpful to me?'

'It helps me,' Vivian says.

'I don't want him watching,' Tanya says.

'You don't mean that,' Vivian says, standing up with a groan. Her knees must be playing up again. Tanya feels a sting of guilt at waking her up. Light creeps round the curtains. Vivian'll have to be up soon for work.

'I do mean it. I just want to sleep,' Tanya says, turning over so that she's facing the other way. It was either that or reach out to her mum but the ball in her chest won't let her do that. She did that in her dream and look what happened.

Vivian walks across the room, treading on the creaking floorboard by the cupboard, then walks back. Tanya feels the weight and warmth of a blanket placed on top of her and then a light touch on her head. 'Sleep well, precious,' Vivian says. There's worry in her voice.

'Night, Mum,' Tanya says.

Vivian closes the door softly and shuffles back down the corridor. Tanya's not sure, but she thinks she hears her crying in the next room.

Tanya leans over and picks up one of the books by the bed. She'll read through to morning, that'll stop any more nightmares.

The words run and jump on the page as if playing leapfrog with each other. She'll just get some rest. Not sleep, she can do without sleep. She'll lie down and close her eyes for a few minutes. If she sleeps, maybe the bad dreams will stay away.

Tanya feels herself slip into sleep. A dream spins round her, she can't quite see what's happening but it doesn't matter as she's wrapped up and warm. She feels something brush behind her and whisper something. It's a girl's voice. What is she whispering?

Tanya looks down in her dream. She *is* wrapped up and warm. In a web that clamps her hands to her legs so that she can't move. She can't see the spider that winds it tighter and tighter around her. It's squeezing the breath out of her lungs, making her exhale every last bit of carbon dioxide. The girl's voice grows louder, stronger, as Tanya gets weaker. It's close to her ear now.

'Wake up, Tanya,' she says.

Tanya wakes up, sweating. She turns on the light and gets out of bed. There's no way she's going back to sleep again tonight.

CHAPTER EIGHTEEN

SENTIENT NIGHTMARES

'"LEAVE NOW", laid out on the worktop like some kind of Ouija pasta. No wonder you were terrified,' Ram sneers. They're outside during break. The indie kids are keeping to the shade, sweating under blue fringes. Three members of the football team kick a ball back and forth, waiting for Ram.

'Like a séance in a spaghetti factory,' April replies. She laughs, Ram joins in. Tanya turns away.

'Tell me you took a photo.' Ram goes to grab Tanya's phone out of her hand.

Tanya holds it to her chest. 'I was trying to get out of the house of horrors at the time, not thinking of Instagram.'

'You weren't thinking at all,' Ram says. 'You could've put it up on the urban myths site, in case anyone had seen the same thing but, oh no, you were too scared. April gets concussion and is back in class the next day, you can't even investigate properly.' He shakes his head and goes off with the footballers.

'We could go back and see if it's still there?' April says, watching him leave. It's hard to tell if she's serious or not. Sometimes Tanya suspects April of deep levels of irony that even she can't detect.

'We might have a problem in going back,' Tanya says.

'Why?' April asks.

'I went past this morning – yes I know,' she says as April opens her mouth to speak. 'It's not exactly on my way to school. I may have deviated. Anyway, I went past and saw that the workers are all over the front garden, knocking down the back gate to get equipment through. It'll be hard to just wander in.'

'They have to go away sometime,' April says.

'Not according to this,' Tanya says, taking out a clipping. 'Local newspaper this morning.' She unfolds it.

REYLAND DEVELOPERS SEEKS NIGHTWATCH STAFF AT SHOREDITCH SITE. MUST HAVE

EXPERIENCE, REFERENCES AND A SCEPTICAL
MIND. applications@constantineoliverltd.co.uk

'A sceptical mind?' April says. 'Is that normally a
requirement for a guard? You'd think a nightwatcher
would need to stay awake and have a high boredom
threshold, not a strong grasp of the scientific method.'

'Nightwatcher. I like that,' Charlie says, walking up
behind them. 'Sounds like the kind of gender-neutral
superhero I'd like to be.'

Ding, ding, ding.

They all get messages through at once.

'Classroom. Now.' It's Miss Quill. Usual lack of
courtesy or explanation. She'd be terrible at meeting
the queen. Tanya's aunt went to meet the queen at a
Buckingham Palace garden party. She said the sandwiches
were very nice although a bit thin on the ham and that the
lawn was so green it could be fake, which is the highest
praise for her – nothing was so great that it couldn't be
faked better. Her aunt said that when the queen asked
her 'And what do *you* do?' she couldn't think and just
answered, 'Zumba, Ma'am. On Tuesdays at 11. Come
along, if you like. It's good for the knees. I've got spare
leggings if you want them.' The queen seemed keen but
never showed up. Lightweight.

They move towards the door. When Miss Quill calls, you don't even question it. When shadows can attack, who knows what's going on in the classroom at any moment?

The classroom, though, is empty. At least it looks empty. Miss Quill emerges from the stationery cupboard, clutching a pen.

'I thought I'd lost this,' she says, holding the pen up high and staring at it like she was checking a diamond for faults. 'I once signed the death warrant of a king with this.'

'Finding a pen in a stationery cupboard. That must be the most surprising thing ever to happen to you, Miss Quill,' Tanya says, sitting down in her usual chair.

'Sarcasm is beneath you, Tanya. It's why they call it a "chasm".'

'But it's not spelled—'

'And it's probably not just a pen,' Charlie says. 'It's some kind of special device.'

'Now you've made it sound like a dildo, Charlie,' Ram says. 'Well done.'

Charlie splutters, trying to cough out a denial.

'We need to talk about your urban legend site, Ram,' Miss Quill says, quickly switching focus.

'It's not mine, I only—'

'Found it, yes. But you've added to it, haven't you.' The last sentence most definitely wasn't a question. Miss Quill can even out-eyebrow Ram.

He looks away from her gaze, which, to be fair, was one of her uncomfortable ones. Like putting on a scratchy jumper and then being unable to get your head back out of the hole.

Miss Quill brought the site up on the screen and clicked through to the right page. She was right. There were two new entries, the last one put up last night by 'Striker'.

'I don't know what to be more disappointed by,' Miss Quill says, 'the fact that you posted about what happened at the house yesterday without discussing it with us first, or you calling yourself "Striker". Could you not have chosen something more effervescent in its wit? Have a dash of panache in your online persona if not your everyday one.'

Ram shrugs. 'Doesn't bother me.'

'What does he say?' Charlie asks.

Everyone leans forward, trying to read it from the screen.

'Look it up if you want the details,' Miss Quill sniffs. 'The thing I'm interested in is that this wasn't the first time he posted.'

The others turn to look at him.

'What?' he says. 'Am I not allowed to write online any more?'

Miss Quill scrolls back to the previous post that went up just before they met up last night. She zooms in and highlights a phrase: 'Faceless Mary stood in the window. A mouth appeared in her blank face and she started to scream. We could hear her over the rush of the wind, it was chilling. If we hadn't run then, I don't know what would've happened. My friend was lucky I was there.'

'Oh, I was, was I?' Tanya says.

'Yeah,' Ram says. 'You were.'

Tanya folds her arms and breathes out slowly and loudly.

'The point is,' Miss Quill says, using her pen to point out exactly what and where the point is on the screen, 'that the legend of Faceless Mary is alive.'

They look at her blankly.

'We all saw her, the girl with no face, whose mouth morphed out of her head as she came towards Ram. Right?'

They all nod, apart from Ram, who shrugs again. He's good at shrugging.

'But that wasn't part of the urban myth until Ram wrote it. That wasn't what happened when you went yesterday, according to what you both told me. It wasn't a case of the girl having no face, you imposed that *after* you'd read about her. Basically, you made it up, probably to impress people. Suddenly, though, she's pursuing us as if she were like that all along. Writing her like that *made* her like that.'

'How can that happen?' Tanya asks.

'Legends have their own life and get passed on, they're contagious,' Miss Quill says. 'They evolve, shifting with each host. It's how culture grows. Where would we be without the enduring stories of Parsela and Whitshade?' A wistful look crosses her face.

More blankness happening.

Charlie turns round to explain. 'They're rebels. From our planet. I mean they weren't real but—'

'They are real to those who believe in a republic. They are as real as any story with truth running through its centre,' Miss Quill says. She stands military straight, shoulders back. Tanya can almost see Miss Quill's old world revolving around her, then fading as she comes back to this one. 'What's different in this case is that she, and the other creatures, were tangible.'

'Maybe it's because the house is so near the Rift?' Tanya says. 'Maybe all stories need is a source of external energy to make them live.'

'That's a theory at least,' Miss Quill says.

'Does that mean it's growing in strength?' Ram says. Nothing in his voice says he's worried. The frantic tapping of his fingers, however, does.

'It's possible that you've helped a sentient nightmare to evolve, Ram,' Miss Quill says.

'And as sentient nightmares go,' April says, 'it seemed very keen on you.'

'But who spelled out the pasta?' Tanya says. 'Wouldn't Faceless Mary want us there to add to her dust pile collection? Why would she want us to leave?'

'Contrary Faceless Mary?' Ram says.

'So what do we do about it?' Charlie asks.

'We don't have to do *anything* about it,' Ram says.

'We *could* be doing more harm than good by being involved,' April says. 'Ram should write a post saying that Faceless Mary and her Magically Morphing Mouthparts have left the house and then the living legend will die. Won't it?'

'I don't know if it works like that,' Miss Quill says.

'Then how does it work?' Charlie says. 'We can't get into the house because of the developers. And, anyway, how do you fight a legend?'

'By getting to its source,' Miss Quill says.

CHAPTER NINETEEN

MR ALAN F. TURNPIKE
OF MEADOW ROW

'Why do I have to be here again?' Ram asks when Tanya walks up to him and April at Elephant and Castle Tube station. 'Charlie and Matteusz aren't.'

'Can you stop moaning for just a minute?' Tanya says.

'No,' Ram replies. Then he smiles.

Miss Quill strides over. 'Follow me,' she says. She walks out of the station with Tanya, with April and Ram trailing after her.

There's a slight breeze. It was so boiling in the underground that, when Tanya missed the first Tube, she'd been grateful for the rush of coolness and bit of grit in her eye.

'Nice place you've brought us, Miss Quill. Don't they call it "Effluent and Castle"?' Ram says.

'If the people who live here call it by that name, that's one thing,' Miss Quill says, 'anything else is propaganda. Always ask, who profits?'

'Why do I get the feeling we're no longer talking about Elephant and Castle?' Ram asks.

'Very perceptive. There's hope for you yet, Mr Singh,' Miss Quill says.

'Was that sarcasm, Miss Quill?' Tanya says. 'Because sarcasm is beneath you, that's why—'

'Thank you, Tanya, that will do.' It's unclear from her face if Miss Quill is pissed off or pleased, but then that's normal. Her phone vibrates. She takes it out, looks at it and frowns. 'Charlie and Matteusz won't be joining us,' she says. 'Charlie says they're onto something.'

'Sounds interesting,' April says.

'Sounds suspicious,' Miss Quill replies, walking off. The others follow a few steps behind. She strides past a street full of tiny shops running by the station. It smells of garlic and rosemary, cinnamon and batter. Tanya's stomach rumbles. Miss Quill marches on. No time for a snack, then.

'Remind me why I'm here again?' Ram shouts over the traffic.

'You said you'd keep me company,' April replies.

'And I am, aren't I? So what's our plan of attack?'

'There will be no "attack",' Miss Quill says as they go under the bridge. 'Tanya tracked down the person who runs the site, we're going for a friendly chat.'

'I've seen your "friendly chats",' Ram says.

'And you'll be the recipient of one very shortly,' Miss Quill says. Even her bob has an angry swing. Angry bob.

Meadow Row may well have been a meadow once, filled with cornflowers and butterflies, boxed-in by hedgerows, but now it features low-rise '70s-style blocks surrounding a patch of green. A few trees rustle around the edges of the grass. Trees always seem to know something. They're like a group of girls that you always think are talking about you.

Mr Alan F. Turnpike lives on the top floor of the nearest set of flats. As they climb the stairs, Miss Quill says, 'Leave this one to me.' She looks with distaste at the door knocker in the shape of a ghost and knocks with her knuckles instead.

A man in his forties, fifties maybe, hard to tell, opens the door. He pushes his glasses up his nose. Seeing Miss Quill, he swallows twice, opens his mouth to speak, then closes it again. It's like she's a word stealer.

'Mr Alan F. Turnpike?' she says, looking straight at him. Her bob shimmies.

'Yes?' he says.

'Don't ask me, tell me. Is that your name?'

He steps backwards, his hands coming up to his chest. 'Er, yes?'

'Miss Quill, I think you're scaring him,' April says, tapping Miss Quill on the shoulder.

Miss Quill flicks April's fingers from her without even looking. 'I'm not scaring you, Mr Alan F. Turnpike, am I?' she asks. 'Because that would not be edifying for a man of your renown, stature and experience now, would it?'

Mr Alan F. shakes his head. A lot.

'Right then. So we'll come in and talk about it, shall we? Yes? Good.' Miss Quill walks into the hallway of his flat, motioning with a switch of her bob for the others to follow. Alan F. stands flat against the wall, nodding at each of them as they pass through into the small lounge. Black patches stain the walls like squashed spiders.

Miss Quill sits in the armchair, perching on the edge of the seat. Her back is so upright it's as if her spine's been put through straighteners. 'Sit down, then, Alan,' she says, patting the chair next to her.

He walks forward, apologising to Ram and April as he passes. He plumps up the cushions on the sofa and makes sure that all the Blu-rays are lined up on the shelf. Ram and April sit on the sofa, Tanya on the chair at the desk crammed into the corner. Sitting down next to Miss Quill, Alan looks round the room, his eyes baffled wide. 'Can I ask, if it's not too rude a question, what you're doing in my flat?' he asks.

'Alan,' Miss Quill says, 'I may call you Alan, may I?'

'Of course,' Alan says, 'Al, if you like.'

'Well then, Alan, and I will call you Alan, if I may, it's a beautiful name, it means "handsome and helpful one" in at least three languages.'

'Does it?' Alan says, sitting up a bit taller himself. His back cracks and he slumps again.

'I'm sure of it,' Miss Quill says, utterly believably. 'Anyway, what I *would* like to talk about is Myth City.'

He turns as pale as milk. 'I've already called a solicitor. I'm not supposed to talk about it.' He stands up. 'Can you leave, please, I don't even know why I let you in.'

'And you should ask that question of yourself more thoroughly when we've gone. Now, however, we just want to talk with you, that's all,' Miss Quill says. 'We may even be able to help.' She's got her reassuring voice on, as if talking a cat down from the top of a cupboard. 'Why do you need a lawyer?'

Alan places two fingers in his mouth and chews on his nails like they're nubs of corn on a cob. 'There's a story on my site that some developer's claiming is lowering the value of their property.' He breathes slowly in and out.

'I'm not making it up but they say it's a malicious attempt to undermine them.' He laughs. 'I couldn't be malicious if I tried.' Tanya gets the sense that this is so true that even if he *did* try it would be like a kitten putting on boxing gloves. 'Thing is, this developer's persuaded my employer to give me the sack. I think they've worked together on something. I'm unemployed because of that house.'

'It wouldn't happen to be an old stone house?' Tanya says. 'In Shoreditch?'

Alan turns to her. 'Why? What do you know?'

'We've all been to the house,' Miss Quill says calmly. 'We know that it's true. Well, that some of it is true. Ram has posted twice himself. If the developers want to get nasty, they can call on Striker.'

'Thanks, Miss Quill,' Ram says. 'Good to know you've got my back. So glad I came.'

Alan leans forward, staring at Ram 'Really? You're Striker?' His face lights up. He now seems much younger. 'She screamed at you?'

'You seem more invested than someone who just runs a site,' Miss Quill says. 'You've been there, haven't you?'

He nods, shuffling his feet. 'I first went years ago. There were loads of rumours about it when I was at school and I've always been into that kind of stuff.'

'Which school?' April asks. She looks completely innocent. Tanya tells herself to never play high stakes poker with April. Or Miss Quill.

'It was Coal Hill, wasn't it?' Ram says. Tanya tells herself to play high stakes poker with Ram as soon as possible.

Alan nods. 'I don't know what made me go but one day, a day like this actually, hot, muggy, storm on its way, I found myself walking home that way. That's the first bit I can't explain, there are many others. I never normally went that way but I felt compelled, as if drawn to it on some level.'

Tanya feels the others staring at her. She doesn't look at them. The same thing happened to her and she doesn't know how to explain it either. The nearest she can put it is that it was like walking towards an unseen lighthouse. A darkhouse.

'I stopped when I walked past and looked up. It was, as usual, in shadow. There was a young woman standing in the top left window. She put her hand up to the glass and I couldn't tell if she was waving to me or warning me away. I couldn't see her face at all.'

'That could have been someone who lived there,' Tanya says.

'The only person who lived there was an old woman. A widow. Her husband died years before and she didn't have a daughter, a niece, anybody that would fit the description of a teenage girl. I was convinced that the old woman had trapped her there, either that or—' He stops. When Tanya looks up, he's staring at her.

'You've seen her, haven't you?' he says to her. 'I can see it in your eyes.'

Tanya tells herself to never play face-to-face poker with anyone, ever. It's easier online – a poker face is easier to keep when you don't have one. 'What are you saying, that she left some kind of mark on my retinae? Bit too J-horror, even for me.' If you don't know how else to play, bluff.

'Whoever I've talked to about the stone house, it's the same thing – they felt called there. Even if they meant to go somewhere else, they were somehow compelled towards it. And they are all similar in some way.' He looks away. 'Lonely, lost or have lost.'

Silence. Thick, embarrassed silence. A soupy kind of silence, a minestrone with bits floating in it that you can't, and don't want to, identify.

'That could describe anybody,' Miss Quill says, briskly, brushing her hands. 'It's like palmistry. I could tell anyone's fortune, even if they didn't have a palm.'

'Really?' Alan asks. He touches his palm, subconsciously or not.

'Oh, come on then,' Miss Quill says, taking his palm in her hand. 'Right.' She traces a few lines on his hand and looks deeply into his eyes until he tears his away. 'You're a sensitive person who has known loss and sadness, you find it hard to let people know the real you but inside you're aching to be known. You are thinking of moving on but something is holding you back. If you don't address whatever it is that has a hold on you, then you will be stuck forever.' She looks up. 'Accurate?'

'Wow,' he says. 'Just, well, wow.'

'Exactly. You could say the same of any human being, of any being at all.' She stops, thinks. 'Well, that's not quite true. You wouldn't say that of a Dalek, would you, unless you wanted to provoke them into killing you and why would you want to do that?'

'Um. I wouldn't?' Alan says. He is staring now at Miss Quill with eyes so soft and squishy he could be looking at a baby panda gif.

Miss Quill sees the look. Tanya swears she can see the catlike calculation cross Miss Quill's face: play with Alan or don't play with Alan. Claws in or out. She places his hand back in his lap and pats it. 'No, you wouldn't. Alan, you really don't want to dally with predators.'

'No,' he says, looking strangely disappointed. The UST in the room is confusing.

'Can we get back to the stone house?' Tanya asks. 'You know, the reason we're here?'

'I did whatever I could, you know,' Alan says. 'I called the police and even went in a few times. The old woman found me digging around in the attic and flew at me. It was like one of those ghost train witches who fly over your head, only she just launched herself at me.'

'So more like an elderly lady reacting to you breaking into her house?' Tanya says, her tone so dry it could soak up all the mould in the flat.

'She was definitely angry. Said she didn't know how I dared to enter her house. It was sacred, she said. I asked her what she meant but she started crying, rocking backwards and forwards, holding this weird doll with a hat on.'

'There's a room full of foreign dolls,' Tanya explains, as if that's a normal thing to say.

'I saw it. Really creepy. Where did she get them, that's what I want to know? She never went anywhere as far as I can work out,' Alan says. 'Anyway, I went back once after that, late at night. I could hear the old woman snoring in her room so I thought I'd be safe. A bit of me thought that maybe *she* was the young woman in the window, dressed up *Psycho*-style.'

'That would be insane,' Ram says.

Miss Quill shrugs. 'People do a lot more insane things,' she says.

'So I looked into her room to make sure it was her snoring and not a tape or anything like that. I've seen films, I know how things work, and there she was. Not a bolster in the bed, no pulley system, this wasn't *Ferris Bueller's Day Off*: the old woman was asleep. And Faceless Alice appeared by her bed. She stood next to the old woman and stroked her hair. Then she turned to me, her face like an oval moon and reached out. I ran out of there so fast and I've never gone back.'

'So what do you think she is?' April says, huddled up with Ram on the sofa.

'Honestly?' he says. 'A ghost. I can't think what else she could be. She's why I started the site in the first place, to see if any one else had seen her. And they have. Lots. I've had reports come in steadily ever since. Given that I never found the girl and she seems to be exactly the same, twenty plus years later, the same again before that, I can only conclude that she's an apparition.'

The silence is now sad and weighed down.

'What are you going to do about the legal situation?' April asks. She's taken out her notebook. She'd make a great barrister one day. To be fair, she'd make a good anything. That's probably what her report says from every teacher – 'She'd make a good anything, now take her away and get her to stop asking questions, I'm tired.'

'If I don't take the site down,' he says, 'they're going to sue. I'll probably never find out who she is, or why she is now screaming.'

Miss Quill stands up to leave. 'Thank you for your help, Alan,' she says. 'It was illuminating. If we find anything out about Alice, we'll let you know.'

Alan nods and looks as if he wants them all to stay. He doesn't ask.

Miss Quill turns back when they reach the front door. 'What does the "F" stand for?'

'Fergus,' Alan Fergus Turnpike says. He blushes. 'Does that mean something in several languages as well?'

Miss Quill sucks her lower lip. 'Let's just say, you should never go to the Eckbear system,' she says.

'Why not?' he asks.

'Having the name "Fergus" means you will leave with neither clothes nor dignity,' Miss Quill says as they start walking along to the stairs.

Tanya looks back. Alan Fergus Turnpike has a look of wonder on his face that suggests he now longs for the Eckbear system and will google it within the minute. 'He looks lost here. You don't think we should just send him through the Rift and see what he finds?' Tanya whispers.

Miss Quill considers this then shakes her head. 'We all have our own Rift,' she says. 'He'll find his in time.'

Tanya watches her, still not sure if Miss Quill is joking.

CHAPTER TWENTY

THE FIRST VISIT TO
CONSTANTINE OLIVER

'He won't be much longer, I'm sure,' says Matteusz. 'Can I get you anything, Miss Quill?' he asks.

'I'm fine,' Miss Quill says, folding her arms. She's in the lounge, waiting for Charlie to get home. Why do people in this country call it the living room when they just sit in it, watch television and wait for death?

'Then I'll go upstairs,' Matteusz says, backing out.

'Seeing as you refuse to tell me where Charlie is, I think that wise. I wouldn't want to enact my coercion techniques.'

'I wouldn't want that either,' Matteusz says. He runs up the stairs much quicker than normal.

A key turns in the lock. Charlie comes in whistling. Miss Quill turns off a show in which people try to guess what other people haven't guessed, which must be a war training programme of some kind. Those who win are most likely enlisted by the government as military strategists.

'Come in here, Charlie.'

Charlie walks in, eating a burger. 'I couldn't wait till dinner,' he says. 'I was starving.'

'You're always "starving",' Miss Quill says.

'You'll know why when you hear where I've been.' He sits down on the chair opposite.

'I cannot wait,' Miss Quill says.

Charlie leans forward. 'I went to Highgate, to Constantine Oliver's offices, the stone house developers.' He shows her the advert.

'And why would you do that?' she asks.

'Let me tell you what happened, first.'

She leans back on the sofa. 'Do you have to?' she asks.

'Yes,' he says. 'The whole place looked exactly like an office someone called Constantine Oliver would have, all polished and shiny and nothing on any of the surfaces apart from a coffee machine. You'd have liked it. I felt like I shouldn't even be walking on the floor, it was so clean.'

'Maybe you shouldn't,' Miss Quill says.

'I was shown into a side room and waited. It took so long that I worried they'd worked out that I'd completely made up the CV and references but Oliver came in, eventually. He didn't even bother looking at me, all he said was that he was surprised that I had applied for the job, given my age and that no one from the reputable firms had gone anywhere near. I didn't need to pretend that I didn't know what he was talking about, because I *didn't* know what he was talking about. I asked him why I wouldn't want the job.'

'Not the interview technique Coal Hill careers officers usually recommend,' Miss Quill says. 'What did he say?'

'He said, "Let's get this straight, I've had men, supposedly grown men, try to do the nightwatch onsite and run away screaming. I'm looking for people not easily spooked." I told him that I was his man and asked what I should be looking out for.'

'Oliver then told me this story. Apparently, anyone who's been there after midnight, any time really between 12 and 3 a.m, sees monsters. Really hideous monsters that seem to crawl out of the walls.'

Charlie nods. 'Others have seen creatures made out of bones. The worst part—'

'As if that wasn't bad,' Miss Quill says. Bones do useful things like stop a body from flopping on the floor; bones by themselves is a sign that something's amiss. Combine bones and monsters and you're in nightmare territory.

'The worst part,' Oliver said, 'is that the webs wrap themselves around whoever is inside. They wake up as if coming out of a trance and find they are cocooned in sticky cobwebs that have to be sliced through with a knife.'

'Knives *are* required. You see, that's why I'm always right,' Miss Quill says.

'I'm hoping that'll come across on the phone,' Charlie says, grinning. 'Because in about five minutes, Constantine Oliver is going to call you for my reference. He's all but promised me the job. The last bit is down to you.'

'And I'm supposed to tell him what a fine, upright citizen you are?' she says.

'Tell him that you wouldn't be where you are right now without me,' Charlie says.

'That's true enough,' Miss Quill says.

Her phone goes.

'That'll be him,' Charlie says, expectantly.

'I don't like you assuming that I'll help you. Or that I want to.'

'Please?'

She presses OK. 'Mr Oliver,' she says. 'I've been expecting your call.'

CHAPTER TWENTY-ONE

A TOUCH OF WIST

Tanya settles on her bed, pillows behind her, textbooks laid out in front. Nothing too taxing before bed, she's just relaxing with some hot chocolate, three-dimensional trigonometry and a touch of Bragg scattering for fun.

Her phone goes. It's Charlie on FaceTime. His slightly pixelated face appears. 'Nice pyjamas,' he says. 'Are those unicorns?'

'At least I'm wearing pyjamas,' Tanya says. Charlie rolls his eyes, grabs a T-shirt from his bed and slips it on. 'You're home then. Miss Quill is not happy with you.'

'We'd have been no use going off to Elephant and Castle with you so we used our initiative instead. I say *our*, it was mainly *my* idea.'

'I *am* here, you know,' Matteusz says, out of shot.

'That's why I said it,' Charlie says, smiling across to the other side of the room. Matteusz appears from the left and kisses Charlie on the neck.

'I wish people would say if they're in the same room,' Tanya says. 'I might've said something rude about you.' She pretends to think for a moment. 'Thinking about it, I'd say it to your face as well so it doesn't matter.'

'I'd expect nothing more,' Matteusz says. He then kisses Charlie again and moves away. She can hear him on the far side of the room. His shirt is thrown over the bed, covering Charlie's head and the phone.

'So where've you been, then?' she asks, when Charlie stops laughing.

'Nosy, aren't you?'

'You called *me*, remember? I was looking forward to some time *not* looking at your faces.'

'Fine. If you don't want to know what we found out about the stone house, we'll go.'

'Tell me now or I'm going to turn you off and go straight back to my homework.'

'There's no better way to turn me on, but okay. Well, *Matteusz* had the great idea—'

'And it really was great,' Matteusz says.

'Matteusz had the OK idea to find out more about the developer.'

'That *is* such a good idea,' Tanya says, 'that I did the same thing earlier. You needn't have called after all.'

'Ah, but did you go down there after class and have an interview, pretending to apply for a job on the site?'

Tanya shakes her head. 'Can't say I did. Mainly 'cos I can't be in two places at once.

'Charlie can,' Matteusz says, looming into view and winking.

Charlie punches him lightly on the shoulder. 'No, it just *feels* like I can.' He's smiling. He looks so happy.

'I have no idea what that means,' Tanya says. 'And I don't want to.' She wouldn't say she was wistful at the sight but definitely wist-ish. A touch of wist, perhaps. She picks skin off the top of her hot chocolate and drapes it over the other side of the cup. 'So what happened?' she asks.

Charlie repeats what he told Miss Quill, adding some insults for good measure.

'What did you say to him when he talked about the house being haunted?' Tanya asks.

'This is the best bit,' Matteusz says from off screen.

'I made suitably sceptical scoffing noises,' Charlie continues.

'Do the noises,' Matteusz shouts. 'I've been making him do the noises all evening.'

115

Charlie demonstrates the scoffing – he sounds posh and incredulous.

'When really you were scared witless when you were there,' Tanya says. 'I saw your face.' She takes a slurp of hot chocolate and grimaces. She drank from the wrong side of the cup and now has a milk-skin mouth.

'I don't want to go back,' Charlie says. 'I don't want to see any more. I wish we'd never gone but it's in my head now. When I go to sleep I've got images of our war in my head, *and* someone else's. I've caught someone else's nightmares.'

'Maybe the nightmares *are* viral,' Matteusz says.

'Whatever they are, I think the only way to get rid of it is to face it.'

Tanya doesn't know what to say to that other than, 'It's true.' It's the only way she'll free the girl from the window and from her head.

'If what Oliver says is right, you'd think there'd be lots of mummified bodies gift-wrapped in webs,' Tanya says. 'I mean, there were a *lot* of webs in the house, you'd expect them in a place like that, without anyone living there, or a cat to eat the spiders.'

'That's true,' Charlie says. He pauses. 'Unless there is somewhere in the house that we haven't explored. We were pretty much chased out of there.'

'You're right. We should go again,' Tanya says, jumping up. Her books slide off the bed onto the floor.

'What?'

'What?' Matteusz echoes Charlie, appearing on screen in a dressing gown.

'Let's go right now. Miss Quill has some of those EMF readers they have on *Most Haunted* and prove, well, something at least.' She's carrying the laptop around the room, holding it up while trying to find warm clothes.

Matteusz and Charlie haven't moved. They're staring at her through the screen.

'Aren't you going to get dressed?' she says.

'You're basically saying you want us to be ghost busters,' Charlie says.

'I'll be Kate McKinnon,' Matteusz replies. 'She has the best hair.'

'Charlie, what are you waiting for?' Tanya asks.

'I'm waiting till it starts,' Charlie says. He swallows. He looks nervous. Matteusz's hand appears and holds on to Charlie's.

'When what starts?' Tanya asks.

'I got the job as nightwatcher at the stone house. Starting tomorrow.'

CHAPTER TWENTY-TWO

DREAMWEAVING AGAIN

Tanya knows she's dreaming. She'll wake up now, right? If she's having a *really* great dream, then realises she's asleep, she always wakes up. Consciousness steps in like the party police and switches off the sound system. But now, when she's dreaming of ivy crawling out of the walls of the stone house and wrapping itself around her and pinning her hands behind her back, she can't wake up at all. She pinches the skin of her other hand. Hard. Nope, still dreaming.

Don't panic. It's only a dream. A dream that is making her heart beat so hard it feels like it's reverberating through the stone walls.

She's read about how to wake up from nightmares:

1. Concentrate

Concentrating on specifics should shift her brainwaves from theta to gamma and beta and jolt her awake. Right. Let's try this. She looks down and focuses on the vine grabbing her arm. It's as muscular as a snake and squeezes her as tightly as the python she held at the aquarium when she was five. Fine wires spike out of the dark green flesh. They latch onto her skin, making her itch and bleed. But not wake up.

2. Observe

Look for things that aren't part of ordinary life. This should, in theory, alert her brain to the fact that she's not in an everyday situation, but if 10 metre strands of ivy strangling her don't appear unrealistic to her brain, then not much will.

3. Scream

Asking for help stimulates the amygdala and sends the body into survival mode, causing adrenaline to flow and the eyes to fly open to assess the threat. Tanya concentrates on opening her mouth as wide as she can and screams. 'HELP'. The sound that comes out seems muffled. Any second now, though, she'll be awake. Any second.

4. Blink

She tries really hard to blink. Closing your eyes and opening them in the dream can cause the body to do it in real life, letting light in on the dreams, like opening the curtains. It's impossible. Her eyelids won't move. It's as if they've been sewn shut with steel thread.

5. Run

It's hard to run when a plant is squeezing you like a green corset. There's no way her actual body is going to kick out and wake up if her dream body can't twitch.

6. Listen

She hasn't read this anywhere, but she's got a theory. Tanya waggles her hands to try and get more leeway, just enough to touch the wall behind her. It is cold and slightly slimy. Forming her hand into a fist, she strains to knock her knuckles against the wall. Her brain is in R.E.M and has a certain rhythm, if she switches it to the bass heavy beat of alpha then she might wake up. She hits out a steady beat against the walls. THUD, THUD, THUD, THUD, THUD... The house responds, wrapping her hands in vines until they cannot move at all.

Tanya's all out of strategies. The ivy loops itself about her neck, tightening its grip. She rasps, raking in each breath.

Can you die in real life if you die in a dream? Has that actually been proven? Now wouldn't be a good time for Tanya to test it. Not for Tanya, anyway.

The edges of her vision blacken like an X-pro II filter. Around her, sounds of scratching. Tendrils slither across her mouth, gagging her. She bites, it squeezes tighter. The dream turns grey.

Soft footsteps cross the floorboards. A hand reaches out, touching the coil around Tanya's neck. 'It's alright, Tanya,' the girl's voice says. The ivy strands slacken. 'It's Amira.'

Tanya's eyes jolt open.

She's in her bedroom. Tanya gulps down air like water. She waits for her heartbeat to slow to sprinting pace then picks up her tablet, types in 'MISSING PERSONS CALLED AMIRA'. Google is her friend. So, it seems, is Amira.

CHAPTER TWENTY-THREE

RUNNING BY THE RIVER

I wake up, not screaming for once. I was dreaming of Tanya. She was helping me clear the garden of all the overgrown ivy. My cheeks hurt from smiling in my sleep.

I slip out of bed and look out of the window. Bright sunshine already, even though it can only be nine in the morning. Men are laughing in the garden. My hands ball into fists. They're sitting on the wall that they've half torn down. Others are erecting a cabin under the trees. A tent has been put up next to it. I do not want to see another tent. Why would people live in them if they didn't have to? When they have houses and loved ones who aren't dead inside them?

I hear people laughing and wonder who will get hurt.

We were at the last camp, in Calais, and the worst. We'd travelled through ten countries and now that we were so close to England, it looked like we'd never get there. There was little or no water in the camp. We couldn't clean ourselves so we couldn't pray. Yana and I slept on one board with a thin blanket over us both, in a tent shared with twelve members of a family from Homs. I can't even say their name. It makes my throat close up. The tent was partitioned into different areas and we had our own 2 metre by 2 metre tarpaulined space. It wasn't real privacy, though. One night we were sleeping and two of the sons came into our area of the tent. I woke up with a hand over my mouth. They were laughing, pulling at my nightclothes. Yana curled up in a ball. I kicked at them and they laughed more, grabbing my feet. The tarpaulin rustled aside and their father appeared. He shouted at them and they left, still laughing. I held Yana to me and we both rocked backwards and forwards. Next morning, we were told to leave the tent.

I used to love making people laugh – Father called me his 'little clown'. So much about me has changed. One time, I was really good at running and jumping and playing. Yana and I used to race each other by the river. We went from one bridge to the next, which is a very long way, especially for someone as young as she was. But she always managed, sometimes even had time to stop to pick a flower on the way. She shouted at me for letting her win but she was so fast that she won all by herself. I should have told her. If she visits me tonight, I will tell her. And I'll say sorry. For that and other things.

The Stone House

The digging has started outside. They're churning up the lawn and its beautiful overgrown roses and dandelions. Seeds bob outside the window then get caught up in the wind and taken away.

The house is unhappy. It creaks and moans. Doors cry shut and walls shudder. I tell it that everything will be okay. I used to tell my sister that. It wasn't okay. The house knows this and sheds autumn leaves from the ceiling. I remember autumn in Damascus. Yana used to love holding hands with me and Baba, scuffing at the leaves. I even have vague memories of doing it myself, very small, wearing a raincoat. Memories are one way to keep off the rain. I curl up back on the bed, hoping to be covered in leaves.

CHAPTER TWENTY-FOUR

PHENOMENA

Tanya is waiting at the gates again. For Miss Quill, this time. At least *she* won't be late.

It's slightly cooler today, although maybe she's just getting used to it. The headlines in the corner shop still shout 'HOTTEST EVER!', showing packed British beaches and close-ups of smiling white girls.

She didn't fancy eating before she left home this morning so bought something that claims to be 'breakfast in a can'. She takes a swig. Tastes more like freshly squeezed dirt in a can.

'I sincerely hope you're not waiting for me,' Miss Quill says, striding towards her.

'Bad luck,' Tanya says.

'Then my hope is misplaced,' Miss Quill says. 'Such is the way of visionaries.'

'You're my hero, Miss Quill,' Tanya says.

'I'm glad you recognise it,' Miss Quill replies.

'Have you got the results yet on those samples?' Tanya says, stalling for time.

'I should have by this evening. Next question.' Miss Quill looks towards the window of the staff room.

'I'm not sure it's a question, exactly.'

'What do you want, Tanya?'

Tanya reaches down and picks up the huge paper cup of coffee. 'It's a bribe. I'd like your help.'

'Of course you do. What else do you lot ever want? What if I say no, what're you going to do then? Sort it out by yourself, that's what.' Miss Quill takes a long drink and closes her eyes. After an uncomfortably long time, she opens them again.

'Well go on, then, what do you want?'

'I had a dream last night where the girl in the house told me her name.' Tanya looks at her shoes, not wanting to look Miss Quill in the eye. She can do without disdain today.

'And?' Miss Quill says, not a trace of contempt in her voice. Tanya looks up. Not a sign of it on her face, either.

'Amira. She said her name is Amira.'

'Have you checked the missing persons' register?' Miss Quill asks.

'First thing I did. There are three Amiras reported missing in London,' Tanya says. 'Two of them in their teens, which is the nearest I can guess her age.'

'Followed up on them?'

'One has been missing for a long time, several years. The picture is from when she went missing so she'll probably look different now, although I was too far away to get any kind of look at my Amira's face.'

'*Your* Amira?' Miss Quill's eyebrows lift.

'You know what I mean, the one in the house.' Tanya blushes but doesn't know why.

'And the other lost Amira?'

'I found her on Missing Kids. She's twelve. It may be her, might not be.'

'And you want to know what to do next?' Miss Quill asks.

'I want to know that I'm not going mad,' Tanya says quietly. 'Basing an investigation on something I heard in a dream is not exactly scientific. It's not something you'd teach in physics, for example.'

'There are lots of things I don't teach in physics or anywhere else,' Miss Quill says. 'We know so little about dreams and how they work, even where I'm from. Nightmares and dreams are a complex processing mechanism, an alchemical composite of memory and emotion. You said, after the last time you went, that you thought you heard her say something.'

Tanya nods. 'But I didn't hear what.'

'Maybe you did,' Miss Quill says.

Tanya returns to staring at her shoes. 'I was wondering whether there's some kind of connection between us,' she says. 'I keep being drawn to the house and seeing her.'

'I wouldn't be surprised. There is something very powerful about that house.'

'Have you felt the same thing?' Tanya asks.

Miss Quill drinks more coffee. Looks at her watch. 'Time you went inside, Miss Adeola.'

'But Miss…'

Miss Quill is already hurrying across to the entrance, fingers clamped round her coffee cup.

Tanya spends the day keeping an eye on the time. The hours pass as if the hands on the clock are coated in blackstrap molasses. Her stomach rumbles. She could do with some of her mum's molasses and ginger cake. She could take some tonight, say it's for the sleepover at April's that she's using as a cover story. They should probably sort out what April's doing for a cover story.

It's alright for Charlie and Matteusz, Miss Quill knows what's going on most of the time. Mainly because everyone is too scared not to tell her. That and the fact she's often the one leading them into something.

Tanya looks back up at the clock. Is it going backwards? Could be. Round here, anything is possible.

The others aren't as worried. Ram has already said he's not coming along tonight and even April said she'll only come if she's finished her essay. Matteusz is only going because Charlie is supposed to be working at the house. Miss Quill is going because Charlie reminded her that it's her responsibility to look after him. The only one who seems bothered is Charlie. He's sitting in front of Tanya now, checking his watch as much as she is, but probably wishing it would go backwards. That's probably why it seems so slow, it's stuck between wanting to please him and her.

The hand drags forward another tick.

Tanya knows Amira's there. Whatever the police say, and she's bothered them again today, she can feel it in her bones. Bones she'd like to stay wrapped in periosteum and blood and skin and not used to make up the limbs of a monster, if you don't mind. She had to stop herself going there in the middle of the night by herself, told herself over and over that they would go tomorrow. That the girl in the window would be OK for another day. But what if she isn't? What if that time before the developers descended was the only window for getting Amira out from behind hers?

When Tanya went to the stone house in her dream last night, it was as if she were there. She might as well *have* been there and seen the nightmares for real and then maybe they'd be further on.

'Excuse me, Miss Adeola. Would you mind joining us for a second?' Miss Quill is standing in front of Tanya's desk. Her eyes flash.

'Sorry, Miss Quill,' Tanya says. She looks down and realises she's been doodling. The picture is of a girl, standing in the window of an old house.

'I'm sure that whatever you are thinking about is far more interesting than quantum phenomena but do try and stay with us.'

'Not at all, it's, er, phenomenal,' Tanya says, wishing she could either disappear at her own embarrassingness or hit her own head against the desk without it a) hurting and b) looking weird to an entire classroom. She settles for a silent, mouthed 'sorry' to Miss Quill.

The slightest hint of amusement dances across Miss Quill's face. There was definitely a hint of a twitch of a smile around her mouth.

'See me, afterwards, would you, Miss Adeola?' Miss Quill says before walking to the front of the class and tapping her hand against the screen. 'Right. Those who have been paying attention will have no problem answering this past paper question linking the photoelectric effect and ionization, will you?'

April just about stops herself from clapping her hands. The rest of the class groans.

Miss Quill's mouth twitches nearer a smile. 'That's what I like to hear,' she says. 'Happiness.'

When the bell goes, Tanya walks up to Miss Quill's desk. Miss Quill holds up her hand as she marks the paper on top. 'Why do they always find these topics difficult?'

'Because they link work function to electrons escaping from individual atoms,' Tanya says, leaning against the desk. 'It's a basic error.'

'You may have a firm grasp of physics, Tanya, but you're not so hot on rhetorical questions, are you?'

Tanya stares at her, not answering.

Miss Quill shoos Tanya off the edge of her desk.

'What did you want to see me for? Is it about tonight, because if you think we shouldn't go, I—' Tanya asks.

'Are you alright?' Miss Quill interrupts. Her face is scary without any sarcasm on.

'I'm fine, why do you ask?' Tanya can't quite look her in the eye, her gaze fixed on the blunt edge of the Quill fringe.

'You're distracted in class, you've hardly answered any questions, you look as if you haven't slept since you found the stone house.'

'I *have* slept. Just not very much or very well,' Tanya says.

'I've been thinking about it. If you *are* connected, with this girl or the house, then maybe you shouldn't go at all. You are, after all, only fourteen. I sometimes forget that I'm not dealing with soldiers,' Miss Quill says.

'I'll be fine,' Tanya says, wishing she'd never said anything to Miss Quill.

'The Prince is also sleeping badly, hardly eating. He is far too bothered by something he saw at the house.'

'He saw things from the war but I don't know what it was in particular that disturbed him. It must have been when I went back into the kitchen.'

'And I was busy with the others,' Miss Quill says.

'Pretty impressive that he's scared but still going back in as nightwatcher,' Tanya says. 'He's facing something, I don't know what it is but he's staring it down. I wish I could be more like that.'

'You can't let these things creep under your skin,' Miss Quill says with disdain. 'If you do, they start to change you.'

'How do *you* stop getting involved with things? Your students, for example? Or even Charlie?'

'I never get involved in the lives of my students or my charges.' Her tone is Brillo-pad brusque.

'Of course you don't, Miss,' she says. 'Can I go now?'

Miss Quill nods, her brow furrowed. 'See you at 11 p.m.'

'And you'll have the equipment?' Tanya says.

Miss Quill rolls her eyes and waves her away. Tanya looks back to see her holding her head in her hands. She looks tired, as if she's not sleeping either. Maybe that's what she was trying to say, in a Quillish way. Maybe it's not just Tanya and Charlie that the stone house has affected after all.

CHAPTER TWENTY-FIVE

CONSTANTINE OLIVER LTD

Miss Quill walks around the reception room of the Constantine Oliver offices. Swiping a finger across the desk reveals not one spot of dust. The espresso machine shines as if never used. A place this clean must have something dirty to wash away. It's the antithesis of Alan Turnpike's flat and the worse for it.

Through the door is, she supposes, Oliver's office. The blinds are shut. A printer purrs inside.

'May I help you?' the receptionist asks, looking up from his Facebook page. The name tag on his lapel says 'Rajesh'. His suit probably cost more than a month's wages. She was right to wear the power jacket and pencil skirt combination that matches her hair.

Miss Quill buttons a smile to her face with her dimples. 'Good afternoon, Rajesh. A pleasure to meet you. Wonderful office,' she says.

'Thank you,' he says. 'It takes a lot of upkeep.'

'I can imagine. I hope your hard work is appreciated.'

Rajesh's arched left eyebrow shows that it really isn't.

'Well, it doesn't go unnoticed by me,' she says.

'Did we talk on the phone?' Rajesh asks, looking down at his notepad.

'That's right, I'm representing Alan Turnpike,' Miss Quill says. 'I'd like to see Mr Constantine.'

'As I told you on the phone, Miss...' Rajesh waits for her to tell him her name. She doesn't. 'Mr Constantine doesn't take unsolicited meetings. If I can refer you to our own legal team at...'

The door opens. A man with a young face and silver hair strides through the door. He walks as if his feet have never touched the earth. 'Is there something I can help with, Rajesh?' he says. His voice is as smooth as a polished banister. Oliver gives her the eye-flick, up and down, and smiles. Less silver fox than silver piranha.

Rajesh starts to speak. 'I'm sorry, Mr Oliver, I was just asking her to—'

'I can take it from here, thank you, Rajesh. Tidy the place up, would you? It looks fit for the wrecking ball in here.'

Miss Quill and Rajesh exchange glances that Constantine Oliver is too vain to interpret.

Oliver ushers her through. 'Sorry,' she mouths through the glass. Rajesh shrugs and smiles.

Constantine Oliver's office continues the sleek and sheeny theme of the reception. Pristine glass shelves feature one item each – a vase with no flowers, a portrait of his family without him in, a business award in the shape of an iceberg that has been polished so many times that parts of his name have been rubbed off.

'Thank you for seeing me,' Miss Quill says.

'Always happy to help. Our motto here at Constantine Oliver Ltd is "Serving the Community" and we must live up to our promises, mustn't we?'

'Mr Oliver,' Miss Quill says.

'Call me Con,' Oliver says.

'You don't think that's an unfortunate name for a business owner?' Miss Quill says.

'Not at all,' Oliver says. His smile doesn't drop. It's as if it's been stapled to his face, although it'd be hard to find a stapler or anything useful in here. There are no filing cabinets, no drawers. Even his desk is one sheet of glass resting on metallic poles. 'I like to think that it conveys informality. I want my business friends to be relaxed.'

'Right,' Miss Quill says, sitting down on the hardest sofa she's ever encountered. Her prison bunk was more comfortable. She places her bag on the glass table in front of her. Oliver twitches slightly.

'Now, how can I help you?' he says as he settles behind his desk and stretches out his legs.

'I'd like to discuss the flats you're building on the Shoreditch site.'

'Ah, you want to buy one, do you? Well, that's very good to hear, very good indeed. Getting in early, are you? Very shrewd. It's a wonderful time to buy. Prices still going up. How can I make this a pleasant experience for both of us?' he asks. She'd very much like to stop him smiling. But not yet.

'I'd like to see the layout, please. The estate agents said that as the flats weren't officially on the market, they couldn't give them to me.'

Keeping eye contact with her, he presses a button on his desk phone. 'Rajesh, would you please bring me a copy of the blueprints for the Shoreditch site?'

The sound of drawers opening comes from next door. Rajesh comes through with a large sheet of paper.

'Lay it out on the small table,' Oliver says. 'Thank you, Rajesh.'

Rajesh moves Miss Quill's bag to one side then smoothes the plans out in front of her. He gives her a bewildered look, then leaves.

'As you can see, we can offer you an array of one - and two-bedroom apartments, all of a very high specification.'

'How many of them are already sold?' she asks.

'Let's just say you can choose where you like, I like to give special customers priority.'

'Do you mean that no one else has bought yet?'

'You would be the first to get your hands on the blueprint. We're in a very exclusive buying period.'

'Then I am so glad I came today,' she says. She doesn't know how he manages to look so cheerful. Charming is tiring. And very suspicious in others. 'What is the time scale for the build?'

'We'll be pulling down the existing building in the next few days and excavating the foundations by the end of the month. Our intention is to integrate the beautiful and historic stone in the existing house into the new property to give it the authenticity that this company represents.'

'Historic?' Miss Quill says. 'Did someone noteworthy live there, or maybe it's the site of a famous event?' She opts for the April-esque innocent face.

'Well it's old, it's certainly part of history,' he says, faltering very slightly.

He carries on quickly. 'We want to get as much built before winter, with a view to opening in spring. This time next year, you could be sitting in your very own exclusive property, courtesy of Constantine Oliver Ltd.'

'May I keep this?' she says, already folding the blueprint. 'I'd like to decide which one and need to take my time.'

'Of course,' he says. 'Although I should warn you that the price will be going up in the next few days, once we have broken ground.' He looks so convinced that he might even have fallen for his own lies.

She places the blueprint in her bag. 'I'll bear that in mind,' she says. 'There's just one potential issue that I can see.'

'One we shall smooth out, I hope,' he says.

'I hear there has been some trouble on the site. That it is difficult to get staff due to rumours about what goes on inside the existing building?'

'Oh no,' he says. 'None of that is true. No, no.' He moves the singular piece of paper on his desk half a degree to the left.

'It's not true that there are rumours?'

'I don't believe so. And even if there were, which there aren't, Constantine Oliver Ltd only deals in the very best sites. There'd be no truth to them. You must remember their source: they spring from feverish imaginations and people who have their own agenda. Some people don't want more expensive flats in the area, they want affordable housing but that is relative, is it not? The only thing rumours *really* damage is the intelligence of those who believe them.' He smiles even wider if that were possible. Not one flaw in his teeth.

'But there aren't any rumours?' Miss Quill says.

'No, no. Nothing to worry about.'

'With that assurance in mind and on tape,' Miss Quill says, tapping her bag, 'I'd like to discuss your letter to my client, Mr Alan Turnpike.'

No shift in the smile. His teeth could act as a homing beacon for alien civilisations. 'You said you were here with a view to purchasing a flat.'

'No, you said that, Mr Oliver. Sorry, Con,' Miss Quill says.

'Mr Turnpike,' Oliver says, 'has been causing us significant trouble.'

'And there I was thinking you were causing *him* significant trouble. Causing him to lose his job in a charity.'

'All we at Constantine Oliver Ltd did was to inform Mr Turnpike's employers of his activities. What they chose to do with that information is nothing to do with us.'

'His site has been running for years. He hosts ghost stories and urban legends, he's not libelling you or hurting them in any way.'

'I think you'll find his scaremongering has led to forty different employees leaving the Shoreditch site. It's been blacklisted by several agencies. It took long enough to get planning permission, I do not have time to waste on retaining superstitious staff. I think you'll find I have other projects.'

'Will you be able to prove that this is a direct result of my client's website?' Miss Quill asks.

The smile slides a few centimetres.

'Because I'll be interviewing every single one of them and presenting their evidence.'

'I think you'll find they'll say the same thing – that the site scared them away. There are also potential owners of the flats I'm building prepared to say that after reading his alarming stories it put them off purchasing.'

'I'm sure you can get people to say anything you want them to, given enough money and flashes of your teeth.'

The smile vanishes. He's the Cheshire Cat in reverse. 'Are you implying that I'd bribe people? I do hope not. That would be slander, as I'm sure you're aware, Miss...' He pauses. 'I don't believe you told me your name, let alone showed me your credentials.'

'You never asked. Showing great interest in your potential client, aren't you? It's true, I did none of these things and I am implying that your case is extremely weak. *I* think *you*'ll find that my client is not worth your attention. I'm sure you never intended to see any of your threats through.'

Oliver stands and comes out from behind his desk. The veins stick out on his forehead. For one moment, she sees something flash through his eyes that reminded her of someone she met back home. A general. She shakes it off.

'I don't want anyone unauthorised on my property,' he says. 'It's private. I'll do with it as I wish, as is my right. Any evidence that he's inciting trespass and I'll show you exactly what threats are.'

'I think you'll find you just have,' Miss Quill says. She picks up her bag, then bends and places a hand flat on the glass table, leaving a print from which a palmist could tell her fortune. She suspects her fortune, given by the look on his face, does not include a birthday card from Mr Constantine Oliver.

CHAPTER TWENTY-SIX

NIGHTWATCHING

The street is quiet, as if every house, block and person is waiting with them, holding a collective breath. The cat from the playground passes, tail switching. It stares at the house.

'Are you sure you're alright?' Ram whispers to April. 'You could just drop us off and pick us up later. Or stay at home – you did have concussion.'

'I'm not letting you have all the fun,' April says.

'You call being in the same place as this lot "fun"?' Ram says.

'Alright then, I'm not letting you have stories to tell without me,' April replies.

'I thought you weren't coming,' Charlie says.

'If it were up to me, I'd have left you to it.'

'I persuaded him,' April says, linking arms with Ram.

'Sssh,' says Tanya.

The front door of the house opens. A man comes out, locks the door and checks several times that it's secure. Hurrying down the path, he looks back to its black windows and pulls his jacket tight around him. He walks quickly away, whistling loudly.

No one speaks. He hurries past them without acknowledging them in any way. A phone vibrates, making Matteusz jump.

'Charlie says we can go in,' he whispers, looking down at his phone. 'He's asked if we've brought any food.'

'I've got molasses cake,' Tanya says, holding up her bag. She'd told her mum that she needed a whole one. She wishes she hadn't now. It's really heavy. And she'll have to share it.

Miss Quill walks up behind them. She's wearing a fleece, a rucksack and huge sunglasses. She looks like a spy masquerading as a backpacker. Looks like the rucksack is the nearest they'll get to a proton pack. 'I want it known now,' she says, 'that I am here in order to make sure Charlie does not die as that would not end well for me. I am *not* here to babysit any of you. Do you understand?'

'Perfectly,' Tanya says.

'Good. I hope someone has arrived here with a plan,' Miss Quill says.

'Check the readings; see what effect the creatures have other than scare us witless; find Faceless Alice,' Matteusz says, as if ticking items off his 'Unassailable Plan' checklist. He walks round to the boot, opens it and takes out a stepladder. 'And climb a ladder.'

'Can we not call her that?' Tanya says. 'Her name probably isn't even Alice. Don't jump to any conclusions about any of this.'

'Good advice, Tanya,' Miss Quill says and, just as Tanya is about to look smug, 'make sure you follow it.'

'Do you have the results back yet on those samples, Miss Quill?' Tanya asks.

Miss Quill nods. 'I got them just before I came out. I had to go and collect them. That's why I'm late. The dust is carbon based but contains traces of elements that aren't known on earth.'

'So they *are* alien, whatever these things are?'

'All I know is that the dust features unknown elements. None of which is known to my planet either. That wasn't the most interesting result, though,' she says. She takes out her binoculars and looks up at the top window but says nothing.

'Go on, then,' Tanya says.

'What am I supposed to go on?' Miss Quill says, looking puzzled.

'What's the most interesting result?' April jumps in, her tone one of utter exasperation.

'Oh,' she says. 'I'll tell you inside.'

Tanya's got to hand it to Miss Quill: she knows how to wind people up.

As they walk up to the stone house, they hear a key in a lock. Then another. Charlie's right on time: he said he'd let them in when the evening guard left. The front door opens. It's surprisingly quiet. The door to an old stone house should creak a bit, sigh at least, if not give out a full-scale CRAAAAK. Charlie doesn't appear.

They follow each other in single file down the path, Matteusz being careful not to take out plants with the stepladder. He needn't bother: the workers have trodden down most of the plants; wildflowers and weeds all flattened to the ground; dandelion clocks stopped, their seeds lost to the wind.

Tanya feels a tide of sadness, as if coming in waves from the house. Don't jump to conclusions, she tells herself.

In the doorway, Miss Quill digs the torches out of her rucksack and hands them out. Ram shines his torch under his chin. 'Woooo,' he says to April.

She shakes her head in despair and laughs at the same time. 'Does that ever get old?' she asks.

'Noooo,' he says in the same ghostly voice.

'You are both children,' Matteusz says, squeezing past and walking in. He puts down the ladder and sends light into the hall. 'Charlie,' he calls out.

No reply. His voice carries along corridors.

'Charlie? Are you hiding?' Matteusz says. 'Because there are better times for that.'

Footsteps echo upstairs. Tanya gets a little closer to Miss Quill.

'There you are,' Matteusz says, as the light finds Charlie standing at the entrance to the kitchen. Charlie inclines his head.

'Right,' Miss Quill says. 'Keep your phones on you at all times, just in case. I have some equipment for you all but we should check something first.' She holds out her black pen.

'I told you it was a gadget,' Ram says.

'This,' Miss Quill says, as if it's the most obvious thing in the entire world and they're all unbelievably stupid for not knowing, 'is an artron energy detector. Among other things. It measures the amounts of artron energy in any location. Coal Hill School, for example, delivers a very high result. Anything that may have emerged through the Rift will cause the cartridge to burn indigo.'

She pauses, unscrewing the pen. It looks like an ordinary cartridge inside, one of those that will, at some point in the day, cover your hands, anywhere you *put* your hands, and the pocket in which you keep it, in splodged ink. The cartridge turns bright purple, sending out a lilac glow to her face.

'Artron energy *is* present,' Tanya says, looking about the dark house. Part of her is disappointed, and annoyed at herself. Her instinct is off, she was sure this was not about aliens.

'But not in high quantities,' Miss Quill says, checking a reading on the pen lid. 'We're not dealing with a mass invasion, most likely an isolated case.'

'A lone, lost traveller?' Tanya says, mainly to herself.

'Maybe,' Miss Quill says, 'or it could be a fracture, the creation of the Rift may have caused splinters to occur, like when there's a crack in glass. It doesn't stay in one place. We won't know for sure until we track down the source of the energy.' She sneezes and scratches her nose. 'It seems even more dusty in here than last time.'

'Does it flash brighter when we get near the source?' Ram says.

'This isn't hide and seek,' Miss Quill snaps. 'It won't beep to tell us whether we're "hot" or "cold".'

A beeping sound comes from her rucksack.

'What's that?' Matteusz says.

Miss Quill pockets the pen and looks inside her bag. She pulls out a long black box. The dials on the front are hitting red. She frowns. 'This shouldn't be happening,' she says.

'What?' Matteusz asks.

'Hold it for me,' Miss Quill says, handing Matteusz the contraption. She rummages again in her bag. The beeping gets faster, more frantic.

'What is this?' Matteusz asks, looking closely at the dials.

'An EMF meter. Measures fluctuations in electro-magnetic fields,' she says. 'I brought it as you said you wanted ghost-hunting equipment. I didn't expect it to go off.' She pauses as she reaches further into the rucksack. 'I've got another one, in case that one is broken. Always carry a back-up.' She pulls out another one and turns it on.

Beep. Beep. Beep.

'Could that one be broken too?' Tanya asks hopefully. 'Do you have a back-up for your back-up?'

'Er, Matteusz,' April says slowly. She's using her 'keep calm' voice.

'What is it?' Tanya says. Her heartbeat picks up. If April is using her 'keep calm' voice then there is something to be not calm about.

April's hand rises, points towards Charlie. The torches all land on him. There is something different about his face. It's cold, impassive, as if carved from marble. He stares at Matteusz, lip curled into a sneer. His hand snaps out, holding Matteusz by the throat. Matteusz drops the beeping box, grabbing Charlie's hand and trying to unclamp it from his own neck. Charlie's face is full of hate.

'Stop it, Prince,' Miss Quill shouts, slamming the heel of her palm into Charlie's elbow so that he loosens his grip. 'Now.'

Charlie whips round to face her and throws her against the wall. 'You're next,' he says.

'Am I really?' she says. 'Interesting.'

Ram runs at Charlie, wrestling him down onto the ground. 'I will kill you,' Charlie says to him, calm in a way that April never intended. Their faces are centimetres apart. 'I won't want to, but I will.'

Tanya holds down one of Charlie's arms, feeling him struggle, the sudden strength of him. April, Matteusz and Ram help, all attempting to hold him still. Dropped torches roll across the floor, sending wheels of light around the hallway, creating a strobe effect that freezes Charlie's snarling face into film frames.

'This isn't you,' Matteusz says, his eyes shining with tears. 'Please, Charlie, this isn't you. It's the house.'

'What if he's possessed?' April says, her voice straining with the effort of holding Charlie. 'He'd never do this.'

'He isn't possessed,' Miss Quill says calmly. She folds her arms and leans against the wall.

'What's your problem?' Tanya shouts at her. 'You're supposed to look after him.'

'My job is to protect the Prince, nothing else,' Miss Quill replies.

Charlie roars with rage and struggles free, grabbing at Matteusz. The beeping has increased to one long scream. Charlie and Matteusz are a tangle of limbs in the half-dark. It's impossible to tell who is who. Something moves towards them. Tanya grabs one of the torches from the floor and shines it at Charlie and Matteusz. An arm reaches out for Charlie. As he turns, a hand finds his hate-filled face. He stops. Lets go of Matteusz. A crack appears in his forehead, widening out, splintering into a hundred cracks that run down his neck and his arms. He points at the figure that touched him. Then collapses into dust.

'No,' Matteusz shouts, dropping to the floor and raking through the ashes with his fingers.

'Hey,' the figure says. He bends down into a beam of light at Matteusz's feet. 'It's me.' Charlie reaches out and holds Matteusz, kissing him and stroking him. 'I'm here.'

'But you were, you just…' Matteusz says, looking from Charlie to the pile of dust that was Charlie, or at least used to be or that's what it looked like.

'It wasn't real,' Charlie says.

'It bloody felt real,' Tanya says, rubbing her head from where she was thrown against the stairs.

'But you turned him, or *you*, or I don't know what, into dust,' Matteusz says, pulling back from Charlie. 'Are you the real one or…' He stops talking and looks down at the dust again, as if words can't go anywhere near to touching what happened.

'What do you really think?' Charlie says, lifting Matteusz's head to look him in the eye.

Matteusz holds Charlie's soft gaze, then touches his cheekbones, his neck and his hands. 'I think it's you,' he says.

'I know it's me,' Charlie replies.

'It's a good job I took your advice, Miss Quill,' Matteusz says.

'Which part?' she asks.

'Always bring a back-up. You never know when your loved one is going to disintegrate.'

His nervous laughter breaks the tension, until they hear it echoing round the house far longer than it should. It seems to linger in the top floor, creepy giggles ricocheting between walls.

'What or who was that?' April says, pointing to the small pyramid of ashes.

They all turn to Miss Quill. She stares back at them. 'Don't look at me,' she says. 'I knew when I fought the imposter that it couldn't be the Prince. My head would've exploded if it were the real one. And my head appears to be in position. I have no idea what it was, though. I don't have the answer stashed in my backpack.'

'You've got everything else in there,' Tanya says.

'Can you not find a leader among you?' she says. 'No? Why did I even ask?' She sighs. 'Keep in twos. That may prevent too many deaths by dust doppelgangers. Natural wastage is, of course, inevitable.'

'Well, that's just charming,' Ram says.

'And please, Prince, no going off into corners and turning each other into dust, if you think you can manage that. If you can't, then clear up after yourselves. There are enough allergens about the place as it is.' She sneezes again.

'That's one advantage in being single,' Tanya says.

Charlie lets go of Matteusz and steps forward. 'Who let you in?' he asks. 'I was upstairs when I heard you shouting, came down to find you wrestling me. I had a dream like that a while ago, although that one was a lot more pleasant.'

'We assumed it was you,' Ram says. He looks around the hallway as if the mystery person is going to step out of the shadows and present herself. Tanya's sure it's Amira.

'I'm supposed to sweep round the house every hour and report anything unusual.' Charlie pauses. 'What do you think I should say about this?'

'I wouldn't say it's unusual at all,' Tanya says. 'Not for us anyway.'

'Then let's go and find something really unusual.'

CHAPTER TWENTY-SEVEN

FALSE SECURITY

Miss Quill hands Tanya the extra EMF reader. 'See if that helps you find your girl in the window,' she says.

'Is this handmade?' Tanya says, looking down at a black box with wires sticking out of it, half impressed, half disappointed that they don't have shiny ghost-catching equipment. It's stopped bleeping at least. It was getting annoying.

'I soldered it myself,' Miss Quill replies, stroking the box.

'What should I do if it goes off?' she says. 'I wasn't expecting to deal with actual ghosts.'

Miss Quill tuts. 'Variations in the electromagnetic field do not necessarily indicate the presence of spirits,' she says. 'There are many alien life forms that have a different magnetic resonance. It could even be based on geological conditions – the earth has a pretty strong magnetic field. You'd be in trouble if it didn't.'

'So it could be what's underneath the house?' Tanya says.

'Possibly. They're intending to dig out the foundations. Any tests could have disturbed it.'

'There could be an old graveyard underneath,' Matteusz says.

'Could be,' Miss Quill says, 'many areas of London are built upon graves and plague pits.'

'Just what we need to hear, thanks, Miss Quill,' Tanya says. 'I'll never be able to walk around London without thinking of that.'

Miss Quill frowns. 'Ignorance is not a position of strength. It brings false security. Now. You have a meter reading to do. If you locate areas of fluctuation then that would be a start. Go off with Charlie and Matteusz. Try and be civil. My group is going to try and find the basement.'

'Basement?' Tanya says. 'I thought there were only three floors.'

'Didn't I say?' Miss Quill says, rummaging again in her rucksack and pulling out a blueprint and a map. 'This was the other reason I was late. I obtained a blueprint for the new development and then thought that a map of the house would be useful. I found the layout of the house from when the conservatory was put on.' She thrusts it at April.

April studies it. 'There's a door down to the basement in the kitchen,' she says. 'We missed it before.'

'And you want us to...?' Tanya says, turning to Miss Quill.

'Go somewhere other than the basement. That way if we meet our deaths down there in a horrifying yet, no doubt, noble fashion, you will live to tell the world,' Miss Quill says.

'You think something's down there, don't you?' Ram says.

'What else have you been keeping back, Miss Quill?' Tanya asks. 'And why?'

'Tanya,' Miss Quill says. 'Knowing more than anyone else is one of your defining features. It'll be good to challenge that, won't it?'

Tanya's jaw cranks backwards and forwards.

'I have some suspicions but it doesn't add up,' Miss Quill says. 'There were two types of web present in the sample, one of which is not from this planet.' She holds a hand out to stop Tanya speaking. 'I don't know any more yet. There's still more testing to do. You're going to have to trust me for now.'

Tanya nods. 'OK.'

Matteusz picks up the stepladder. 'Shall we go up, then?' he says.

Charlie shines his torch up the stairs. The meagre light makes it even darker up there. Maybe she shouldn't be doing this. Maybe they all shouldn't be doing this. They're here because of her. April has already been hurt and she's still here, being braver than Tanya is right now. Everyone is being braver than Tanya.

'After you,' Tanya says.

CHAPTER TWENTY-EIGHT

SPLITTING UP

Miss Quill watches them go upstairs. Hush descends.

'Do you think they'll be OK?' April says.

Miss Quill stands up straighter and turns to her and Ram. 'They will be absolutely fine.'

'And now we're a team,' Ram says flatly.

'You needn't sound so unenthusiastic,' April says.

'There are very many places I'd rather be right now.'

'And I can think of places, times and planets that would be infinitely preferable to spending any more time with you, Mr Singh, but this is the situation I find myself in.'

'So,' April says, shining her torch on the old layout. 'We need to find a way down to the cellar from the kitchen.'

'I didn't see anything when we were last there,' Ram says. 'Do you think there's a secret passage?'

'We've got every other haunted house trope going,' April says. 'Why not add that to the list?'

'It'd be good if we found one, though, wouldn't it?' Ram says to her. 'Maybe it's a person behind all of it and they're just running behind the walls and down concealed passageways, setting off projections. Or holograms.'

'You want the Scooby Doo ending,' April says with a mixture of affection and exasperation.

He wanders round the hall, hand outstretched like he's a great director on a film set. 'He or she could have footage that they play to keep people out. Scare them away. What is it you always say, Miss Quill?'

'Go away?' April suggests. 'Or maybe "The excesses of your stupidity are only matched by your capacity to irritate."'

'If in doubt, follow the money,' Ram says.

'So you *have* been listening,' Miss Quill says as they walk slowly down the hall. 'Next time you fail a test I'll know you're being deliberately stupid and/or obtuse.'

'You don't think he's right, do you, Miss Quill?' April asks.

'We don't know anything about the source of these phenomena.'

They enter the room of dolls. The torchlight slides between their plastic faces, making it look as if they're blinking.

'But there is artron energy here, you demonstrated it yourself—'

'With the sexy pen,' Ram interrupts.

April closes her eyes briefly. 'Yes, thank you, Ram. And electromagnetic irregularities,' she says.

'That's also true. But we have to ask, in a similar way to what Ram just said: who has something to gain?'

'Do you know?' Ram asks.

'I know, at least on the surface, who has something to lose from all of this,' Miss Quill says.

'The developer,' April replies. 'Constantine Oliver.'

'Obviously. This isn't doing his project or his bank balance any good whatsoever.'

'But that might be a cunning plan,' Ram says as they move through into the kitchen.

'How?' April says.

'No idea,' Ram says.

Knives glint on the draining board. Miss Quill examines each one, running her finger down the blade. They're as blunt as onions. Onions are good in many recipes but are of no use in a knife fight. Shame about these knives, though. Fortunately, she's brought her own.

'Someone's been here again,' April says, pointing to the different plates in the sink.

'Probably the builders,' Ram says. 'They need to eat, you know.'

'Why would you rather that it wasn't supernatural?' April asks.

'Why would you rather that it was?' Ram replies. They stare at each other.

'This is highly uncomfortable. Could we please move past this awkward impasse?' Miss Quill says.

'I bet you that, at the end of all this,' Ram continues, 'it'll be Oliver or someone we knew all along. I'll lift a mask from someone's head, they'll shake their fists and say that thing about pesky kids.'

'You *are* pesky kids,' Miss Quill says. 'Now be quiet. We need to find this door. Check for an influx of unexpected air.'

Ram looks at April. 'Are you going to pick up on that or can I? 'Cos that's just a gift.'

'Do you really want to test my patience any more?' Miss Quill asks.

Ram looks at her then gets down on all fours.

'A wise choice for once,' Miss Quill says.

April joins Ram in feeling out the edges of the tiles while Miss Quill runs her hands over the walls. They are the kind of cold that feels wet. No sign of any draughts, though, not in the walls or inside the cupboards full of orange canned goods.

April stands and opens the door into the utility room. She looks through. Then back into the kitchen. And into the utility room again. Placing the map on the counter, she points to the kitchen. 'They've halved the old kitchen,' she says. 'The utility room on the layout is really small, and was probably the pantry. This,' she pokes at the wall that divides the two rooms, 'isn't load bearing. It must've gone in after these plans.'

'You do realise you sound like a forty-year-old architect?' Tanya says.

'You're only saying that because I'm right,' April replies. Grabbing a knife from the draining board, she crouches in the doorway into the utility room and levers up the lino. It peels away easily, the glue that once held it to the floor now grey dust. Underneath, placed into the boards, is a door.

'I think we've found the basement,' Miss Quill says.

CHAPTER TWENTY-NINE

THE BED

Tanya starts up the second staircase. The floorboards make a 'craak' sound, like crows with smoker's coughs.

Matteusz stumbles, knocking the ladder into the banister. The sound reverberates. The whole staircase seems to groan.

'Oh great,' Tanya says. 'You've woken up the house. I was hoping we could get a few minutes in without being set upon by something weird.'

'Stay quiet and it might not notice,' Matteusz says.

'That's like saying "Back away from the hungry bear, it might not notice you're carrying a picnic,"' Tanya replies.

'This isn't helping,' Charlie whispers from the top of the second staircase. 'Watch your step at the top, the rug is frayed. I nearly slipped on it.'

They walk through the same corridor where everything kicked off last time. It's as if nothing happened. The door has returned to its place, the walls show no sign of having been through an indoor storm.

'They've got a good housekeeper,' Tanya says.

'Maybe we all suffered from mass hallucinations,' Matteusz whispers loudly. 'I've been looking into it. It's possible. We should be looking out for a substance or a plant that could cause us to all see the same thing. That's if we *did* see the same thing. I know we compared notes but that's hardly a sound methodology.'

'You should say that in front of Miss Quill,' Charlie says, turning round to kiss Matteusz. 'She'd be impressed.'

Tanya says nothing. Mass hallucinations could actually explain this better than most things. A house that causes a group to imagine certain things, to draw them there and back again. But why? What does it want from them?

In the bedroom, once again, everything has been put back where it was. The wardrobe is shut. The chest contains its drawers. The trunk, though, is open, with books stacked inside. The beds have been made up. There's a dent on one of the beds, as if someone is sitting on it.

She walks over to the bed. Heart thumping, she reaches her hand out above the dip in the mattress. She feels, for one moment, something wispy, like fine threads passing across her palm.

'What are you doing?' Charlie says. 'Come and help.'

Tanya stares at that spot for a moment, then turns. Charlie and Matteusz are both balancing on the ladder, trying to push up the hatch. It lifts slightly, then drops.

'Pass us one of the drawers, please,' Charlie says.

Tanya pulls out a drawer. It's full of lace handkerchiefs, all folded. Flowers are sewn onto the corners. Forget-me-nots.

She begins taking them all out and stacking them on the chest.

'Just tip them out,' Matteusz says. 'We haven't got time for this.'

She can't though. She doesn't know why, apart from that it doesn't seem fair. Someone cared enough to spend the time folding, she's not going to disrespect that.

The handkerchiefs now laid on the chest, she lifts the drawer and hands it up to Matteusz. He holds it up, pushing against the hatch. The board lifts high. Charlie stands on the top rung, straining up. He manages to slide back the hatch until they are all looking up into the dark attic.

'I'll go first,' Tanya says.

'But you're the youngest,' says Matteusz.

'So I've had less time to matter and make my mark. You can't argue with that logic. Well, you can but I'm not going to let you. Now climb down and let me through.'

Matteusz and Charlie jump off the ladder. Tanya takes their place, climbing up to the thinnest top rung.

'Now what are you going to do?' Charlie asks.

'Simple,' she says. 'I'm going to beg you to give me a lift up.' Silence. Although not quite. Somewhere deep in that silence, sounding very faint, Tanya's sure she can hear someone crying. Trying to cover it, she says, 'Well, come on then.'

CHAPTER THIRTY

THE CELLAR

The cellar seems to eat up torchlight, absorbing it into the walls.

'It's like a goth's bedroom down here. Everything's painted black,' Ram says, getting up close to the webbed walls.

Miss Quill checks her pen. It's glowing bright purple. The artron levels are getting higher. Or they are getting closer. Maybe they're playing Hide-and-Seek after all. Not good. She only likes playing games if she has devised them, and even then prefers to let others play them to the end.

'Lots more cobwebs than the rest of the house,' Aprils says, holding out her hands. It's as if she's wrapped them in white lace. She rubs them together as if she thinks she'll never get them clean again. 'Particularly in this corner.'

Ram and Miss Quill join her. She's right. One section of the basement is curtained off with cobwebs. They can't see through, not even by shining the lights centimetres away. Miss Quill places her shoe against it and pushes. It's firm, barely giving in to the pressure. Ram presses his palms to the sheet of web. It undulates. It even resists when, extracting his hands with difficulty from the web, he turns round and leans against it. 'It's like a standing-up bed,' he says. 'Good mattress. Firm.'

'Would you stop that, Mr Singh?' Miss Quill asks. 'I don't want to have to cut you out of an enormous web. Too tiring.'

'What worries me,' April says, moving away from the collection of webbing, 'is what would make that, and why?' She walks backwards into an old wooden box. Her torch drops, breaking the bulb. The room dims even more.

'Share mine,' Ram says, moving closer to her.

Miss Quill turns back to the webbed section. This is the heart of it. It must be. Constantine Oliver told Charlie that workers were found in webbing. What if whatever they were up against had taken the girl, Amira, down here, and left her wrapped up to die? Maybe those rumours of children lost to the house were true.

Miss Quill removes her rucksack and takes out her knives, all wrapped up in embossed dark-red leather. She unrolls them and takes out her favourite.

'What're you doing with those, Miss Quill?' Ram says.

'I'm seeing what we're dealing with,' she says. She places the tip of the knife against the wall of web. It shudders. 'Step back.' Ram and April move to the base of the ladder.

Miss Quill presses the knife into the web. It is resisted at first, then pierces through. A scream comes from inside. She cuts deeper, further. Something scuttles behind the web. A scratching sound comes from the walls and then tearing. Ripping.

A hand reaches through the web from the inside. Then another. They pull at the web, stretching it. Miss Quill tries to help, slicing at the web around where the person is trying to get out, trying to ignore the screams of pain coming from within the cocoon.

'Help me,' says a voice she knows. And then she remembers those hands. Hands she held when she was a kid. A friend lost in a war.

More hands appear through the web, one of them tries to take away her knife, another to get her torch. She wrestles them away, only for more to grip onto her forearms and pull her in. Her mouth is pressed against the web. She closes her lips but it's as if the fibres can find their way through.

Arms wrap themselves about her waist. She twists away but she's held fast. The web weaves itself around her, taking away all light and making her long for sleep.

CHAPTER THIRTY-ONE

THE ATTIC

'Can you see her?' Charlie calls up.

'Give me a chance,' Tanya says, shining her torch into the corners. It smells of damp wood and wet dust up here. There's the usual collection of things that generations have left in the attic for the next owner. Boxes and trunks, an old cot, bits of lawn mower. Far less spooky than you'd expect for a house where dolls are left in a room to multiply and furniture cleans up after itself like a creepier *Beauty and the Beast*.

Walking across the attic isn't easy. There are no floorboards, only sheets of cardboard covering exposed struts. The struts run widthways and she has to take a wide step to cross from one to the other, ducking under webs that canopy the ceiling. Water drips down her neck.

There's probably a hole in the roof but it could be coming from anywhere. It's like IP redirection for water: you'll never know its source till the whole web is exposed.

'We're coming up,' Charlie says. She can see his hand grasping for the edge of the opening into the attic. 'Matteusz is going to give me a hand, then I'll pull him up.'

'I wouldn't,' she says. 'There's not much room in here.'

'I don't like you being by yourself,' Charlie says, 'and before you say anything, it's because we've been told to stay together, not because of your age, gender or dress sense.'

'Or because we like you, obviously,' Matteusz says cheerfully.

'I can't see her anyway, or much of anything else.'

'No adverse weather conditions?' Matteusz shouts up. 'Or faceless people?'

'Nothing. Pretty boring, really. I'll see if there's anything useful then come straight down.'

She squats by some boxes. There must be something in there that can help. The first one contains a huge pile of clothes. They look old. Sixties and seventies styles. Moth-eaten and mould-speckled. Someone could probably sell the lot to a posh vintage shop. Places like that probably have special dry cleaning nozzles or a magic hoover that makes it disappear until you get it home and that yellow stain re-emerges under the armpit.

She opens boxes containing records that have been stuck together with some of the drips from the roof; a cabinet of old perfume bottles; more dolls, this time out of national dress and in Victorian dresses; piles of papers. It's brilliant, looking through other people's stuff, as well as sad. Someone loved, wore, played with these things once.

She sits down carefully on one of the cardboarded areas, making sure a slat is right beneath her, then starts taking out handfuls of documents. Maybe something in there will help. Some of them are almost blank, faded with age before they were placed in the box. Faint signs of writing can be seen when she holds each one close to the torch. No way she can do this with thousands of sheets of paper.

'I'm bringing something down,' she shouts from the far corner of the attic. 'Give us a hand.'

No response.

Crawling forward, she reaches for a beam to help stand then crosses the attic, strut by strut. She peers over the edge of the hatch. It's completely dark. She shines a torch down, hoping that they won't be dazzled by it and fall off the ladder.

But Matteusz and Charlie aren't there. And neither is the stepladder.

'Oi,' she shouts down, 'that's not funny.'

179

They're probably hiding under the beds. Or under the sheets, ready to rise up and scare her. 'You can come out now,' she says. 'I need help. There's a box of documents. Could be useful.'

No answer, not even the echo of her voice as if the house is listening so intently it's kept them in its walls. It feels colder. Probably because she's been up there so long. How long *has* she been up there? Possibilities twist through her mind. Time portal? No, the most likely explanation is that they've heard something from downstairs and gone to find out, knowing she was safe in the attic. But why wouldn't they tell her?

She leans further over, stretching out her arm to point the light in every corner. Her jacket catches on a splinter of wood, causing her arm to jerk back. The torch falls through the hatch onto the bedroom floor. At least she can see the place where she can jump down and break her leg.

'Charlie?' she calls out. This is the second time tonight he's seemed to be missing. What if the real Charlie was the one that turned to dust and the fake one attacked Matteusz while she was busy? That doesn't make sense either. 'Matteusz!' she shouts. 'Anyone! I'm stuck up here and I'd like to get down.'

'Hello,' a voice calls up from the bedroom. Tanya knows that voice. She's heard it here before.

'Who's that?' Tanya says, her voice trembling very slightly.

'I told you my name. I can help you,' Amira says, although Tanya can't see her or anything other than a spotlight on the carpet below.

'How?' Tanya asks. 'Can you get the ladder?'

'It's been taken away. The house wanted you up there. It likes you up there.'

'So how are you going to help me?'

'Jump,' Amira says.

'What, and you'll catch me? Then we'll both have broken limbs.'

'You came to find me, didn't you?' Amira says.

'So that means I should trust you?'

'Just jump,' Amira whispers.

Tanya jumps.

CHAPTER THIRTY-TWO

SOMEBODY AT THE DOOR

She's in complete darkness. The one other time Miss Quill has seen such darkness was in a cell. No windows, no lights, sealed doors, food that she couldn't see, delivered in a black box through a black hatch. At the time, she'd at once admired their thoroughness and couldn't wait for revolution when she'd lock up her captors and show them how thorough *she* could be.

She got out of that place, and she'll get out of this one too, if she can only work out where she is and which way up she is. Miss Quill has a terrible feeling that she is upside down in a spider's web.

'Miss Quill?' April says somewhere to the left in the darkness. 'Are you okay?'

'Of course I'm not okay,' she snaps.

'No, you don't look okay,' Ram says.

'How can you say that when you can't even see me?' Miss Quill says.

'We can see you fine,' April replies. 'I think it might help if I just... bear with me, Miss Quill.'

Muted sounds of footsteps, as if April had covered her shoes with velvet. Something tears near Miss Quill's face. 'What are you do–' She stops talking. The darkness has been thrown off, along with a web that now hangs to her left like a discarded bridal veil. The rest of her has been spun round and round, hoisted up and held on her side, making everything in the torch-lit room seem distorted.

'I couldn't tell what was going on but you touched a hand that was reaching through the web.'

'And turned it to dust. Well done, Miss Quill,' Ram says, giving her still trapped hand a high five. He wipes his hand on his shirt.

'Did you see whose hand it was?' Miss Quill asks.

April has the grace to look sheepish. 'As I said, we couldn't really see. We only had one torch and we were caught up in nightmares. Ram saw his leg being—'

'Alright, you don't have to go over it,' Ram interrupts.

'And I was trying to explain to my parents how I failed physics,' April says.

'If you fail physics then you'll be explaining it to *me* first,' Miss Quill says. 'Now help me get out.'

Ram and April stand there, staring at her.

'You really are useless, aren't you? Use one of my knives. And be careful. The last person who messed with my knives only understood their significance when his head was rolling across the floor.'

'Is that true, Miss?' Ram says. His face says he'd like it to be.

'Make sure you don't find out. Football without a head is difficult. Not impossible, of course. Stop gaping and cut me out.'

Ram and April carefully take two knives out of the leather holder and begin the job of removing her from the web.

'Thank you,' she says at last, taking back her knives, promising them that she'll clean them later. She looks back into the hole that's been sliced into the webbing. There's nothing there. No long lost friend, no web-making creature. If these are palpable illusions then they are very convincing.

Covered in webs, her smart suit now looking like a Halloween costume, she moves back to the ladder. The readings on both the EMF meter and the artron pen have dropped. 'We should find the others,' she says, her foot on the first rung. 'So what have we learned?'

'Do we have to do the reflective learning thing every time?' Ram says below her. 'We can fill out an Individual Learning Assessment when we get back if you really want.'

'We've learned,' April says, 'that the apparitions, or whatever they are, can be turned to dust, that we each had separate encounters that meant something to us but that we all could see, and that something is creating webs.'

'Thank you, April,' Miss Quill says. 'Adequate assessment.' She showed a good understanding of the basics of knife work, too – grip, muscle use, letting the knife and gravity do their jobs. Must be her physics knowledge. With training she could be a useful warrior.

Footsteps on the path outside. Lots of them.

Lights shine through panes in the door. Male voices. The door crashes open.

Miss Quill pulls April and Ram into the deepest shadows. 'Time for that game of hide-and-seek,' she says. But there isn't time at all.

Constantine Oliver shines a light at them and smiles.

CHAPTER THIRTY-THREE

AMIRA

Tanya doesn't want to get up. After crouching in the cold attic, it's a relief to be lying on a mattress in the bedroom, covered in a blanket.

'Are you feeling better?' Amira asks. 'You were shaking when you first fell.' Her voice is soft. She places a large camping lantern next to Tanya. Amira looks about fourteen or fifteen, maybe younger. She's wearing clothes that were designed for someone older and bigger. Her sleeves hang over her hands. She has an accent that Tanya can't place.

'Much better, thanks,' Tanya says, sitting up. Her hands are still trembling, though.

'Please,' Amira says, reaching behind her. She turns back with a tin of beans and a spoon standing upright inside it. 'Eat this. That should help. I'd give you one of the sandwiches the workers left, but they've gone rotten already.'

'Do you know why that happens?' Tanya asks.

'The house,' is all Amira says.

Tanya pokes at the beans then remembers the cake. She opens her bag, takes the cake out of its box and breaks off a piece. It's gone dry already but it tastes amazing. Dense with spices and sugar. She gives a chunk to Amira who eats it as if she hasn't eaten cake in months. Maybe she hasn't.

Tanya looks around the room. The mattress she's sitting on has been dragged from one of the beds and positioned under the hatch. Blankets and clothes had been thrown on top.

'Did you do this to break my fall?' Tanya asks.

'Yes.' Amira laughs. There's some sadness in it. 'There's no one else in here.'

'But my friends were. Charlie and Matteusz. Did you see them?'

Amira nods. 'I saw them come in here with you. I was sitting on the bed. They helped you up into the attic and then the house gathered them to itself.'

'You what now?' Tanya says.

Amira's looking at her as if there's nothing odd in what she's said.

'You know that's crazy, right?' Tanya says. She begins to stand up. She doesn't even know Amira. '"The house gathered them to itself?" That's one of the scariest, most ridiculous things I've ever heard and you say it as easily as if talking about taking a walk.'

'If I were to take a walk, I'd speak about it with joy,' Amira says.

Tanya's about to ask why, then stops, just in time. 'Because you've been trapped here for so long.'

'Because of many things,' Amira says simply. She looks straight at Tanya. She has amber eyes that say things that Tanya can't interpret. Amira looks away. She fiddles with her headscarf.

'Where has "the house" taken my friends?' Tanya asks, walking to the door. It slams shut. The lock clunks. There was no key in the lock.

'I told you,' Amira says. 'We're like dolls in a doll's house. The house wants you to stay.'

CHAPTER THIRTY-FOUR

INTRUDERS

Constantine Oliver's smirk is so irritating it's lucky that Miss Quill's wearing handcuffs.

One of the officers turns to Miss Quill. 'I'm DC Carpenter, this is DC Turner. Can we have your name please?' she says.

'This is the solicitor I was telling you about,' Oliver says. 'Apparently she's so intent on protecting her client that she breaks into my property on his behalf.'

Miss Quill ignores him. 'My name is Miss Andrea Quill and these young people are here at my request. I'm their teacher and all fault should lie with me.'

A noise comes from upstairs.

'Is anyone else in the building, Madam?' DC Carpenter asks.

'There's no one else,' Miss Quill says.

The sound of something falling comes from an upstairs floor.

'It's an old house. It makes noises,' Miss Quill says.

'Stay here,' DC Carpenter says to DC Turner. She shines a light up the stairs and follows it.

'Doesn't look good for you, does it Miss Quill?' Oliver says.

Miss Quill turns away so she doesn't have to look at his face.

DC Turner's radio crackles. 'I've got two lads here, tied up in the hallway,' DC Carpenter's voice comes through. 'Possible kidnap.'

'Tied up?' April says.

'Do you need help?' DC Turner asks.

'My bodyguard will assist,' Oliver offers.

'That won't be necessary, Sir,' DC Turner says.

'Not yet,' DC Carpenter says. She sounds breathless. 'They're covered in some sort of material. Like webs. I'd hate to see the spider if this is the web it makes.'

Constantine Oliver's smirk falls. He goes pale beneath his fake tan.

'Spiders?' he says.

'Can you be quiet please, Sir,' DC Turner says, impatience showing in his voice.

'Well, I can see you have this all under control,' Oliver says, nervously looking at the skirting boards.

'Something troubling you, Mr Oliver?' Miss Quill says.

'Not at all. I've got to return to my dinner party. I left in a hurry when I heard that a group of suspicious-looking characters were let into the house. You know my new night guard I presume?'

'He really should sue,' Miss Quill says. 'This house is full of dangers.'

Oliver glares at her and is about to speak when a scuttling sound is heard above them. 'Thank you, DC Turner,' he says. 'If you need anything further, please don't hesitate to call my lawyer. She's a real one, unlike Miss Quill.' He hands over a card and walks out, avoiding the cobwebs.

Charlie and Matteusz appear at the top of the stairs. They're in swaddling made of webs.

Ram takes out his phone and starts taking pictures. 'How's the Prince feeling now?' he asks.

'Don't you dare put any of those up on Mr Turnpike's site,' Miss Quill says.

Ram takes a few more snaps then puts his phone in his pocket. Charlie glares at him.

DC Carpenter holds each of them by the shoulder. 'I found them on the landing, all wrapped up. It took a while to get them upright,' she says. She tries to help them down the stairs. They can only take small steps.

'Miss Quill's got a knife you can use to cut them out, haven't you?' Ram says. His eyes have malice in them.

'A knife?' DC Turner says.

'Lots of them, actually,' Ram says. 'Sharp ones.'

'Stop it, Ram,' April hisses.

DC Turner searches Miss Quill. His eyes widen when he finds the knives. 'I don't think these are legal,' he says.

'What?' Ram says, turning to April, all feigned innocence. 'She's the responsible adult here. Would we all be here without her?'

'We wouldn't be here without Tanya,' Miss Quill says.

'Where *is* Tanya?' April asks.

'There's someone else here?' DC Carpenter says, her voice sharp, urgent.

'How old is she?' DC Turner asks.

'Fourteen. She was upstairs. Charlie and Matteusz were supposed to be looking after her,' Ram says. He stares at Charlie.

'You don't care about her,' Charlie says. They glare at each other.

'Stop it, both of you,' Miss Quill says.

'He's right about one thing,' Charlie says. 'We wouldn't be here without you. You are supposed to protect me and you sent me upstairs to *this*.' He looks down at his wrapped-up form. He seems so serious and looks so ridiculous, that, despite everything, April giggles. Charlie looks at her, wounded.

There is a dangerous silence. Even the police officers look a little embarrassed by it. Eventually, April breaks it.

'Maybe it's best if we keep away from each other,' April says. 'For a while at least. My parents aren't going to let me out of the house anyway, after this.'

'Perfect,' Miss Quill says. Her voice is completely flat. 'That suits me.'

'Anyway,' DC Carpenter moves back up the stairs. 'I'm going to look for this kid. Charge Miss Quill with possession of dangerous weapons. For now.'

As DC Turner cautions her, the others won't look her way. It doesn't matter. She's been alone before. It's the best way. Safest, for everyone.

CHAPTER THIRTY-FIVE

CONCENTRATE ON THE WEB

'Did you see her face?' Tanya says, turning to me. 'When she got stuck on the stepladder and tried to pull her foot away? Angry trout pout or what? She looked like she was posing for a selfie with an ex's new girlfriend. Brilliant!'

'Why is that brilliant?' I ask.

'People who take themselves too seriously are funny,' Tanya says. 'Anyway. We should introduce ourselves properly.'

'Sorry,' I say. 'Telling you to jump wasn't the best way.'

'No problem. It worked,' Tanya says. 'We leapt straight over the awkward getting-to-know-you phase into the saving-me-from-a-broken-neck phase. Very important phase that, for me. And my neck.'

'You're probably right. I was too shy to do anything other than whisper to you last time and tell you my name.'

She holds my shoulder. It is such a solid, warm touch. 'I knew *that* you told me your name. I couldn't hear when I was here. Then I dreamed about it when I got home.'

'The stone house does that,' I tell her, looking around the room. 'It draws you to it then sets up house within you.'

'There I was thinking it was *you* who'd set up house within me. I only came here to help you.'

'But I told you to leave.'

She slaps her hand down on the mattress. 'And I *knew* that was you, too. I. Am. On. FIRE. Next time Miss Quill doubts me I'm gonna remind her of this.'

'Miss Quill is the sharp woman who looks like she hates everyone and everything?'

'She has her bad days too. She's alright. Clever. And, yeah, sharp is the word. Far sharper than that police officer. She didn't even see us when she looked under the beds. What kind of detective does that make her? A rubbish one, that's what. You know who'd make a great detective? Me, that's who. I look great in hats.' She pauses. 'Sorry, I'm nervous. I talk a lot when I'm nervous.'

'Then we balance each other out,' I say. 'I don't say anything when I'm nervous. She didn't see us, though, because she couldn't. Same reason you didn't see me when I was sitting on the bed when you came in.'

'What do you mean?' Tanya says.

I don't want to scare her. She's like my little sister, who acted tough and as if she knew everything, until the day we left and she knew how bad everything could be. She became very quiet after that. I don't want that for Tanya. The house will never let her go, anyway. It will keep those men away from its walls and from us. It likes Tanya, I can tell. The same way that it likes me.

'The house is clever,' I tell her gently. 'It hides people. Wraps them in a cobweb that stops the world from seeing. You can see them, of course, but you're safe.'

'So we were invisible?' Tanya asks.

'We still are,' I say. 'Place your hand ten centimetres above your skin.'

Tanya does so and looks at me. 'Now what?'

'Concentrate on what you're feeling,' I say.

She closes her eyes. 'It's like there's very fine thread or something barely there but slightly fuzzy,' she says. She smoothes her way up above her arm, her fingers brushing against the same kind of gossamer web that the house has wrapped around me since the day I got here.

'That's it,' I say. 'It's protecting you, keeping eyes away.'

'How can we both see each other, then?' she asks.

'I don't know.'

'And what if you don't want eyes to keep away from you? Does the house give you a choice or do you fight it all the time to try and get help?'

'Do you remember when you saw me in the window?' I ask. Of course she remembers. It was only two days ago; it just feels like longer.

'It's where this all started.'

'If I don't want to be invisible, then I brush off the layer of web. It's easy. Although even then, few people look up and, even if they do, their eyes fly over me.'

'I saw you.'

'Yes, you did. And I'm very glad, although I wish you hadn't come here. I don't want my friends in a house full of nightmares.'

'Do you know how they happen?' Tanya asks.

'I wish I did.'

'I've seen several nightmares since I've been here,' Tanya says slowly. She looks as if she's finding it difficult to find the right words. I understand how she feels.

'I've seen your nightmares,' I tell her, shy again. 'I've seen your mum appear, and your dad die.'

'And what about yours,' she says, now that I have set foot upon the path. 'Which ones are your nightmares?'

'War and bombs and shouts in the night; falling houses and people crying; running in the cold; a man walking in a corridor; a dinghy in the sea and not being able to reach it...' I tail off.

Tanya takes my hand. 'And you've been living in the middle of them since you got here?'

'I've been living in the middle of them since I left Syria.'

'When was that?' Tanya asks.

'My father left last year and we followed a while after, when our house was destroyed.'

'You said "we",' Tanya says. 'Do you mean your family?'

'I left with my sister and mum. Then, after my mother died, it was just Yana, and me,' I reply.

'What happened to Yana?' Tanya asks, in such a gentle, caring voice that I can't answer for a moment.

'It's my fault,' I say, only just getting it out.

'I'm sure that's not true,' Tanya says, in just the way that Yana would.

'No, it is. I gave the last of our money to a couple who said they'd get us across the Channel. It cost more so I agreed to work for them afterwards. They seemed kind, then. They smuggled us into the back of a lorry: twenty of us packed into a refrigerator unit, like dates squished into a packet. Only an inch of space above our heads, hardly any room to move. There was a girl next to me who smiled but we'd been told not to talk. We thought it was so that we couldn't be heard when passing through immigration. I think they didn't want us panicking before we'd got in.'

'Oh God,' Tanya says. Her hand goes to her mouth. 'The air.'

I nod. 'The first half-hour was okay, but then it began to run out. Yana started gulping at the air. The girl next to me helped me hold Yana up near the ceiling of the container but her eyes kept closing. I slapped her face–' I stop. Tears have broken into my voice. 'It worked the first time and second but the journey was too long.' I can't say the rest of it out loud. The horrors of the house are nothing to this.

'I'm so sorry,' Tanya says. She is crying, too.

'I couldn't even bury her. They left her in there, with a little boy who hadn't made it. A few of us, including me and the girl next to me, Zainer, were taken to the male smuggler's house. He locked me in a room and told me that I was going to work for him until I'd paid him back. He is the nightmare I get most often. The man who killed my sister, coming down the corridor to attack me.'

'How did you get out?' Tanya asks.

'I was waiting. I stood against the wall so that he couldn't see me. He walked in and I threw the side table at him, hard, and ran out. I wanted to stop for Zainer but I couldn't. No. I didn't. I ran out of the house and stopped for a moment, looking around me. I saw the road sign and then something told me to run. I ran and didn't stop running till I got here and the door opened for me, shut behind me and that was it.'

When I stop, I realise how tired I am. The words had been so heavy inside me, now they fill the room like grey balloons. I can see why people write.

'I'll do everything I can to help,' Tanya says.

'It helps just having you here,' I reply.

She inclines her head, listening. 'I can't hear anything downstairs. We should leave.'

'You can try,' I say.

She crosses to the door and tries it. 'This happened before. We could throw ourselves against it?'

'It won't help,' I say. 'If the house wants you inside, you'll stay inside. You won't be able to leave unless it decides you can.'

'Who does it allow to leave?' Tanya asks. 'You must've seen people go in and out.'

'I have, yes,' I say. 'I think it keeps people here for company. I think the house is lonely.'

'Pretty sick haunted house,' Tanya says loudly as if wanting the house to hear her. 'If it keeps people here long enough, it can make its own ghosts.' She kicks at the door.

'I think it once had a happy family inside it, and wants companionship again, and laughter.' Or maybe that's what I want.

'Ram thought you were a ghost called "Faceless Alice". Have you seen her? She's haunted this house for years, apparently. If it wants to return to a happy family, maybe it's her family that it misses?'

'I have seen a girl wandering around. I thought it was Yana to start with. She never sees or talks to me. She isn't scary though. I can't remember her face but I think I would remember *if she didn't have one. He brought the nightmare of her with him, though. She wasn't aggressive until he came.'*

'Really?' Tanya says. 'So when Miss Quill thought it was a sentient nightmare then it was true, only the house brought it out of Ram's own bad dreams. He must've read about it then dreamed about it that night. Next day, there she is. All we've done since we got here is add our own nightmares to the ones already in the house.' She reaches out to me and touches me briefly. I can feel the barely there web sheathing her skin like lace. She'll be safe from anyone who enters the house tonight, just as the street sleepers who come for the tomato soup will be safe when they rustle in their sleeping bags in the hallway. The house doesn't let them up the stairs, though. Their nightmares wait on the landing and they never go past.

Tanya gives up on the door and walks to the window. I follow. The lights of London wink on and off during the night, as if waking from nightmares and turning their own lights on for reassurance.

The window rattles as she tries to force the lock.

'It won't work,' I say. 'I've tried all the windows. If I manage to crack the glass, then cobwebs appear and bind it together, covering the hole with something stronger than glass.'

Tanya takes out a drawer and throws it at the window. It smashes as it hits the glass, sending pieces of wood flying. A memory creeps up, like a weed through a crack in the pavement, *of hiding when our house was being raided. I try not to push it away as otherwise it'll live in my dreams and in the house.*

A tiny hole has appeared where the corner of the drawer connected with the glass. 'That's a start,' Tanya says.

The web, covering the window like net curtains, begins to thicken. It spreads out around the fracture, each strand reaching for the opposite side of the hole.

'It's already mending it,' I say.

'Have you ever heard of Stockholm Syndrome?' Tanya asks. 'Cos you're bestowing benevolent motives on something that has kidnapped you. Why aren't you raging? Why aren't you screaming at the walls? I can feel it rising in me and I've only been here half an hour.'

'That's right,' I say quietly. 'You've only been here half an hour. I've been here weeks. This may be kidnapping but I've known much worse. Please do not tell me what to feel.'

Tanya is quiet for whole minutes. I've upset her.

'I'm sorry,' she says. 'I have no right to do that. How long have you been here?' she asks.

'I don't know exactly. I try and keep time through a book I'm reading. I read one page every morning when I wake up. I'm on page forty-eight.'

'Forty-eight days? Maybe more? I'm so sorry. We need to get you out.'

'I don't know where I'll go,' I reply.

Do you know where your dad is?'

'No,' I say. 'I don't know if he made it here. I don't even know if he's alive.'

She's quiet again. She sits back down on the mattress. 'So what do we do now?' Tanya asks. 'My mum will be worried if the police are involved.'

'No one's looking for me,' I remind her. 'No one's worried about me.'

'I'm worried about you. We'll find our way home,' she says, holding my hand.

She should have that fantasy, just as I have mine. I don't blame her for not wanting to be here with me. I didn't want to be trapped in here when I arrived. I'd love to walk on grass and see the sky without a webbed window in the way but I can't imagine that happening. For now it feels good to hold another human's hand and it not turn to dust.

CHAPTER THIRTY-SIX

MISS QUILL IS THE NEW BLACK

Miss Quill is in prison, not for the first time, pacing from one wall to the other. The accommodation is comparatively boutique. One of the guards brings her coffee, albeit in a shade of beige that matches the walls. It even comes with a biscuit. Not a very good biscuit: it cannot support a vigorous dunking. There's also a shiny toilet in the corner and a mattress on the bed. It's a thin mattress, and there's no blanket, but it will do. It's not like she'll sleep here. She wouldn't leave herself exposed, that'd be foolish. Besides, there's no darkness, this time round, to seduce her into slumber. In fact, there's too much light. They haven't turned off the strip lights all night. She closes her eyes against the phosphorescent light and the dawn peering in at the high window.

If she's not released soon then she'll have to start reading the writing scratched into the walls. That wouldn't be edifying, although it might be educational.

The kids have gone home, at least. They're not in her charge for the moment. Felicity, her lawyer, told her that they'd all been cautioned but nothing would go on their records. Various parents had stormed in, demanding to know what had happened. At least she didn't have to put up with their whining and endless questions. Charlie's ability to look innocent will have helped, and Ram's charm. As long as April resisted telling the truth, they'd be ok. They'll have come up with a plausible story. They'd better have anyway, otherwise she may be taken away from Coal Hill. She noted that they didn't exactly throw themselves under the school bus to save her. She never wanted to get involved in this in the first place. This is what happens when you stay in one place. She never made herself the designated adult. It's somebody else's turn but here she is, walking back and forth like a seaside donkey. Tanya still hasn't been found. The house had been searched again and there was no sign of her. She didn't turn up at her house, either. She's gone from searching for a missing person to becoming one.

Felicity has been excellent. She should be, for that price, and given the fact that she came so highly recommended by Constantine Oliver. Miss Quill had taken the solictor's card, the one given by Oliver himself, from the police officer's hand and called her. Felicity had had the enormous pleasure, one that showed on her stressed face, of telling Oliver that she couldn't represent him as she was already representing Miss Quill and that would be a conflict of interest. Very sorry. Goodbye.

Felicity had seized on Miss Quill's idea to sue for injury. Charlie was, officially, an employee of Constantine Oliver, even if he was the one who had lied on his CV about everything including Grade 8 piano, and he had been injured at work. The trespass charge against Miss Quill, however, remained.

They'd also confiscated her knives: they said that she had no good reason for carrying them, plus the make may well be banned. None of that's true. Firstly, she had a *very* good reason, just not one that they'd accept and, secondly, it *couldn't* be on the banned list, as the make wasn't known, not on Earth anyway. She'd had to go to a place in Camden Market where items are sold and deals are done with aliens based on Earth and beyond. If the trader was to be believed, and they usually are, the knives were smuggled across timelines. And now the knives were lost to her. They'll languish in police custody until someone from the market sneaks in and steals them, ready to be sold on again

A. K. Benedict

to another alien. Maybe she should have another go at breaking into a prison. Or let them go. It's not the weapon, after all, it's the one who wields it.

Given the state of the police, it's lucky that there are people like Miss Quill around to save Shoreditch, London and the world from ultimate doom and destruction. Not that it's ever appreciated.

A bolt clunks across the door. 'You're released on bail,' DC Carpenter says, leaning against the doorway. 'Your solicitor says she'll be in touch later. And there's someone waiting for you outside.'

Miss Quill runs through the people who'd pick her up at half five in the morning, if her paced timekeeping was correct. There aren't many.

'You are released on the grounds that you're not to go near Mr Oliver or the house or try to intervene in the demolition. Is that clear?'

Miss Quill stands and adjusts her suit. It was worth the stay in prison just to pick every last silk strand of spider's web from her clothes. 'As clear as your incompetence, DC Carpenter,' she says.

Carpenter makes her bunched-up-lip face but doesn't reply. Uniforms can take their toll on wit.

Miss Quill's rucksack is handed back to her along with all her possessions, each now tagged as if in a morgue. It is noticeably lighter without her contraband knives. 'Where's this visitor?' she asks.

The desk sergeant looks up with eyes that have gone beyond caring. Quill doesn't blame him.

'I'm here, Miss Quill,' a man says, out of sight beyond the desk.

Miss Quill walks round. Sitting there, holding a plastic bag in his lap, is Alan F. Turnpike.

CHAPTER THIRTY-SEVEN

Q & A

'What's in the bag, Alan?' Miss Quill asks as she dips into the front seat. His car is a brown Mini. There are M&Ms that are larger and more tasteful.

'I brought sandwiches,' he says. 'I made them myself. Choice of egg, cheese or crisp.'

'What flavour crisps?' she asks suspiciously. It can all go wrong with the wrong sort of crisp.

'Ready Salted?' he says. He holds the sandwiches defensively to his chest, waiting for her response.

'Then we can continue on our journey,' she says, taking one from him. She lifts it up to eye-level. It has an agreeable amount of butter to counteract the salt. She gives it a nod and a bite. She hadn't realised how hungry she was and takes another.

His relieved out-breath steams up the windscreen.

The duvet softness of the bread contrasts with the crunch of the potato. 'Agreeably onomatopoeic, the word "crisp", don't you think?' she says. Her phone bleeps as it receives one message after another.

'Absolutely,' he says, leaning forward to scrub at the windscreen with a rag. They drive off. Not too much traffic on the road.

'My first question should probably have been to ask what you were doing here,' she says. 'So would you like to answer that now?'

'Of course,' he says. 'April got hold of me through my website. She said you might need a lift and some help.'

'Did she now?'

'When I arrived, she was reassuring all the parents that you'd done nothing wrong, that they had, in fact, gone to you for help. Tanya's mum wanted you to be charged with kidnap but she made her back down. I think you should give them all a break.' He glances across to see how she'll take being disagreed with.

'Do you now?' she says, about to launch into exactly why she does not give one Aulian's breath for what he thinks she should do. Then she stops. She folds her arms. Alan *is* giving her a lift after all, and arguing in the early hours is exhausting.

She's got a voice message. From someone who owes her a favour at a lab, one of the few places fully aware of aliens. He's got the results but he can't tell her on the phone, he says. Well, of course he can't say on the phone. It's a liability to even say that he can't say anything on the phone: it very much suggests that he has something to hide.

'We need to make a stop,' Miss Quill says. 'A laboratory in Brompton.'

'A lab?' Alan says. He rubs his eyes.

'That's what I said.'

'Can I ask why?'

'You just did.'

'Please. I'm trying to help,' he says. Even an Alan F. Turnpike, it seems, can reach exasperation point.

'And I'm showing you the importance of precision. It could be vital in what we're about to find out.'

'Am I part of the investigation now?' he asks. He perks up at that.

'I suppose so. But I'll only tell you what you need to know.'

'Otherwise you'll have to kill me, I know,' he says, laughing.

'Oh no, I wouldn't *have* to,' she says. 'I'd *want* to. I *could*, in theory, let you wander off into the world carrying my secrets, knowing that you'll never tell a soul, not even a soul*mate*, as, frankly, you're unlikely to find a soul to mate with, and even if you find the geek of your dreams, he or she or they wouldn't believe you, thinking it another rumour or urban myth that you'd weaved. I *could* do that. But I'd have much more fun destroying you.' She breathes out. 'Thank you for that, I needed the rant. I'm tempted to tell you now, just so that I have a reason to kill you. It would be excellent for my blood pressure.'

Alan stares straight ahead at the road, gripping the wheel. He's not blinking.

She sighs. 'Fine. I'll tell you what you need to know. You'd better be able to cope with this,' she says, then tells him about what's happened, as much as she can without compromising the security of her mission.

Twenty-five minutes later, when they pull into the lab car park, Alan's knuckles are white on the wheel.

'I knew you wouldn't be able to cope,' she says.

'I'm fine,' he says, swallowing. 'Really. I'll wait here.'

She nods, gets out of the Mini and walks towards the lab. There's a light on at a top window. When she gets to the door and punches in the code, she looks back. Alan is still frozen at the wheel, his mouth moving as if going over what she'd said to make it more real.

216

* * *

Miss Quill emerges ten minutes later. 'So what did he say?' Alan asks as she gets back in the car.

'He confirmed something I suspected,' she says.

'You're not going to tell me, are you?' he says.

'I don't usually promote ignorance but in this case I think it best.'

'I have absolutely no idea how to take that,' Alan says, driving off. There's much more traffic now.

'Where would you like me to drop you?' he asks. 'I can go anywhere you like.'

'I would've thought that was obvious,' she says.

'Not the—'

'Yes, the.'

'But I thought you're not supposed to go there? Isn't there an injunction?'

'They *say* that but has it actually gone through yet? I suspect not. And anyway, there are lots of things I'm supposed to do but don't. I don't: eat green things, they taste of weeds; take vitamins, don't trust anything in capsules; wash, overrated nonsense.'

'Right,' he says, nodding.

'I was joking about the last one,' she says.

'Of course,' he says. 'I knew that.'

'Although I never wash clothes.'

'That's another joke, isn't it?' Alan says, looking hopeful.

'Alan, you're going to be absolutely fine,' she says. 'Now drive this dirt-coloured cube faster. Tanya's in trouble.'

CHAPTER THIRTY-EIGHT

THE DOOR

CRAAAAAAAAAK. Tanya wakes up and fumbles for the torch, pointing it towards the door. It's opening. Very, very slowly. She leans up to the other bed and grabs Amira's arm. 'Amira,' she says, 'Wake up. It's letting us out.'

Amira leaps back as if she's been burnt.

'Sorry.' Tanya knows that's not how you treat someone with trauma but they have to move. Now. 'I need you to come with me. It might be playing with us and decide to change its mind. COME ON,' she shouts.

Amira stumbles out of bed. She's wearing a long old nightdress and, with her hair over her face and a lantern in her hand, looks more like a ghost than anything Tanya's seen in the house so far.

Tanya runs for the door and, throwing her weight at it, pins it to the wall until Amira joins her. She's not going to let it keep them prisoner again. Amira takes her hand. They hurry along the corridor. Ahead, the girls who used to laugh at Tanya stand with hands on the hips.

'You really need to sort out your hair, Tanya,' one of them says. 'We're not being funny or anything, just giving you advice. It doesn't suit you.'

'She doesn't need your advice,' Amira says, barging through them, shielding me.

'Cow,' the blonde one says as they pass. She spits at Tanya's face.

At the top of the stairs, a man tries to grab Amira's hand. Tanya swats it away. A woman cajoles from the corner, calling Amira, 'A beauty. A real beauty. Let me put some lipstick on you.' They try and squeeze their way through a crowd of people boxed into the hall, all on tiptoe, lifting their heads as high as they can to breathe. In her peripheral vision, Tanya sees boats bobbing and people screaming, looking over the sides, reaching down. Amira cries out. It sounds like her heart is ripping.

'Leave her alone,' Tanya shouts. She doesn't know how she's not falling over. She can barely see anything except for bullies, boats and someone she fancies turning around and around on the spot but never seeing her like they were stuck in a haunting game of blind man's buff.

She misses a step on the stairs and Amira steadies her. If they weren't propping each other up, they'd both be face down at the foot of the staircase.

When they get into the hallway, the house goes quiet. No one's chasing them. Tanya's heart keeps beating overtime in case they have to run. They are, suddenly, the only ones here. There's no storm shaking the house. No nightmare people.

The quiet is worse. The house is waiting, watching.

It feels like an itch under the skin.

Tanya tries the handle on the front door. 'Of course,' she says. 'Locked.'

'Maybe your friends locked it after they left with the police?' Amira says, hope woven through her voice.

'Maybe,' Amira says, 'but I don't think they did *this*.' She points to the web knitting itself across the door. They're being sewn in from the inside.

'Could you go and check the back door?' Tanya asks.

'It'll be the same. Any access point gets covered over. It's what the house does whenever I try to leave,' Amira says. 'I've stopped trying. It just makes it harder to see outside.'

Tanya goes to check. Amira's right. The back door is choked with spun silk. Cobwebs extend across the glass of the conservatory so that it looks like a giant dreamcatcher. That's exactly what the house is: the dreamcatcher of Shoreditch; where dreams are plucked out of people's heads and preserved. The house is being mummified from the inside.

She pulls at a section of web. It stretches in her grip and other strands join it, wrapping round her hand like a boxer being bandaged for a fight. 'Okay,' she says to the house. 'Stop, please. I won't try and get out.'

The section of web slackens and falls, slithering across the floor.

As she walks back through the room of dolls, one of them falls from the shelf. Then another. She runs out before she's caught in a mass suicide of moulded figures in national dress.

When she returns to the hall, Amira is crouching down, tracing the scratched lines on the floor with her fingers. 'I wish I understood what this was,' she says. 'They might tell us what to do. Like a spell.'

'You think this is some kind of magic?' Tanya says.

'You don't?'

'There *was* a rumour that the old woman who lived here was a witch but that means nothing.'

'It could mean *something*. What if you're overlooking a *something* that could help?' Amira says.

'Women who live differently have always been called witches,' Tanya says. She kneels and brushes her hand over the scratches. 'This is probably where furniture has been dragged out to be sold. Most of the rooms are empty and they wouldn't care about keeping a floor polished when it's about to be demolished.'

'I'm trying to help,' Amira says.

'I know. I'm sorry. Have you seen anything that could've caused it?'

'No, although if there *is* something, it is probably concealing itself, just as it can hide us.' Amira walks all the way around the markings. 'I've looked at it from the landing and from down here. Close up, it looks like lots of very fine scratches with no overall pattern, but from the first-floor landing, when there's enough light, it looks like lots of circles.'

Tanya runs up the stairs. She looks down at the hallway floor. She can see what Amira means. There are shadows cast across the floor but she can see how there's cohesion and geometry to the etching. From up here it's a series of perfect circles.

Behind her, she hears footsteps. A man walks towards her from the end of the corridor and unlocks the door to one of the bedrooms. As he goes in, something crashes down. Seconds later, the same man is at the end of the corridor again. He walks to the bedroom and unlocks it, disappears inside. Another crashing sound. Seconds later, he's back at the far end of the corridor.

'He's there, isn't he?' Amira calls up, her voice shaking.

'He can't hurt you,' Tanya says.

The man walks towards her, unlocks the bedroom.

Amira retreats into a corner of the hallway and sits on one of the sleeping bags, her knees tucked to her chest.

'Do you enjoy this?' Tanya shouts. 'I'm talking to you, house. What have you got to say for yourself?'

'Don't make it angry,' Amira whispers. 'The nightmares get worse.'

'Come on, then, house,' Tanya yells, 'what else can you do? Are you repeating things over and over to send us mad? Do you think we're going to crack? What will you do then, prop us in a corner like mannequins? Have us sat in the conservatory taking tea for infinity? Make yourself a house of bones?'

Something taps on the walls. Tap, tap. Tap, tap, tap.

'You don't like it when people fight back, do you?' She walks down the stairs, calling out. 'You're a coward. I think

224

your defence mechanism is to show people their fears so that they run away. Only we want to leave and you won't let us. Your defence has become an attack.'

TAP. TAP. TAP TAP TAP.

The sound gets louder. It seems to be coming from underneath the floorboards. Something is coming. Scuttling.

Tanya comes to a stop next to Amira. The cobwebs are creeping up Amira's back.

Tanya stamps them down. 'Just piss off, would you?'

'Stop it, Tanya,' Amira says. She stands up. 'Please.' She pulls at Tanya and makes her face her full on.

'I can't,' Tanya says. 'I'm not going to give up like you have. I'm sorry, but you need to fight.'

'You know NOTHING about fighting,' Amira says. Her teeth are bared, her eyes wide. 'You don't know what it's like to put everything into surviving, only for the person that keeps you going to drown in front of you. Your dad died and that's horrible but I left my home when war destroyed my town, crossed Europe, lost my whole family. I've been jeered at, insulted, assaulted and only just escaped. That is not an unusual story for people, I know. I got here. I know how to fight, Tanya, better than you, better than most.'

Silence. The tapping has stopped.

Very light footsteps come from the end of the hall, too far away for torchlight. The footsteps are coming their way. The owner of them steps into the light.

'No,' Amira says, so quietly Tanya almost doesn't hear. It's a girl, younger than Amira but who looks just like her.

'Amira?' the girl says. 'It's Yana.' Yana reaches out. 'Will you play with me, Amira? Will you play?'

Outside, a dog barks. Someone is coming down the path. Probably the police again, searching for Tanya.

Amira looks up and moves towards Yana.

A key scrapes in the lock as if it doesn't quite fit. Tanya makes out some muttering. 'We need to hide,' she says, tugging on Amira's clothes.

'No. Yana might leave,' Amira says. 'I haven't see her this close up since…'

Yana smiles and holds out her hand. Amira mirrors her, stretching out hers.

'Don't,' says Tanya. Turning her own sister to dust would crush Amira.

Amira and her sister touch very briefly, then Yana begins to fade. The rest of the house can be seen through her.

'The house is losing concentration,' Amira says, trying to hold Yana's hand but it now passes through. She's crying silently.

'It knows someone's trying to get in,' Tanya says. Cobwebs twist into the keyhole.

The door won't open more than a few centimetres. It's webbed shut. A penknife appears at the top of the frame, sawing down.

With what sounds like a swift kick, the door opens. Miss Quill slips through. She's alone. She turns on the torch, straight in Tanya's face.

Tanya turns away, dazzled. 'Thanks for that, Miss Quill,' she says. She doesn't know whether to hug Miss Quill or swear at her. She often feels like that.

'She can't hear you,' Amira says. 'Or see you when you're in the web. You need to brush it off, remember?'

'What about you?'

'She's looking for you, not me. I'll only make things more confusing. Quickly,' Amira says.

Tanya briskly strokes the air above her goosebumped arms. Nothing happens.

Miss Quill walks towards the stairs. 'Tanya?' she hiss-whispers, looking up to the second floor.

'I'm here!' Tanya shouts.

'Keep going,' Amira says. 'I'll do your back.' Tanya's shoulders tingle as Amira brushes away the connected silk.

Tanya waves her hand back and forth on any spot above her forearm where she feels the faint resistance of web. In the small amount of light, she can just about see a thin skein of silver float away. It's like rubbing at a lottery card. Miss Quill's torch whips back through the dark, shining at Tanya.

'I hope your arm is joined to the rest of you, Miss Adeola,' Miss Quill says, as drily as if the arm had turned up late for class all by itself and waved from a desk. 'Otherwise I'll have to turn your disembodied limb to dust and that would be tiresome.'

Tanya smoothes off the rest of the web. It's tiring. She's not taking up exfoliation if this is what it's like. She needs energy for other things.

'There you are,' Miss Quill says. She could sound a bit more pleased to see her. She's been imprisoned by a sociopathic building all night, that should get her some Quill love but no, not even a comradely chuck to the chin. 'That was easier than I expected. We need to leave. Now. Before it becomes harder than I expected.'

'In a minute. I need to wait for Amira,' Tanya says.

Miss Quill's eyebrows twitch. 'You found her?'

'She's over there,' Tanya says, pointing to where Amira was sloughing off her own shroud-like covering. Only the slight widening of Miss Quill's eyes shows any surprise at Amira being revealed. It would make an amazing illusion.

She wonders if any magicians use it. Get Derren Brown on the phone.

'If you could hurry up and make your lower half visible, Amira? It may cause Neighbourhood Watch some consternation if they see you floating down the road,' Miss Quill says.

'Neighbourhood Watch weren't much good when she was trapped here,' Tanya says.

'There's no time to be indignant, Tanya. Mr Oliver intends to start knocking the house down today. I do not want a wrecking ball to the face, thank you.'

Just as Amira's ready, the scuttling starts. And the tapping. TAP TAP TAP. And a new sound, a soft shushing along the floor.

Ivy is emerging from the faded wallpaper and weaving towards them along the floor.

Miss Quill grabs them both by the shoulders, propelling them towards the door. 'RUN.'

A band of ivy tendril loops around Tanya, pressing hard into her stomach. Her wrists are cuffed together with tendrils. The ivy is snaking around Amira, too.

'Miss Quill!' Tanya shouts. She gasps as the ivy tightens, breath forced out of her lungs as it drags both her and Amira towards the wall.

Miss Quill runs after them, tearing at the ivy around Tanya but it makes the ivy tighten more. She scrapes her penknife against the plant but it doesn't even spill sap. She stabs it and twists.

Miss Quill is lifted off her feet, thrown backwards by a force they can't see. Her arms grip the frame on either side of the dining room but she can't hold on. Her back arches. She can't hold on any more and flies through, landing hard against the wall. She slumps to the floor, head on one side. She looks like a doll in business dress.

'Miss Quill!' Tanya calls out. 'Can you hear me?'

Miss Quill doesn't move or reply. The door to the dining room slams shut. They're on their own, again.

CHAPTER THIRTY-NINE

BACK TO THE OLD HOUSE

Tanya and Amira huddle together, wrapped in ivy, cobwebs re-gathering around them.

Outside, a truck bleeps its reversing song. Cars arrive. The chatter of builders.

'They won't be able to see us,' Tanya says. 'They're coming to pull down the house and we'll look like part of the walls.'

'We've got to get out,' Amira says. 'There must be a way.'

'You!' Tanya says, remembering. 'You saved me last time.'

'Last time you were held captive by ivy?' Amira says, voice full of disbelief.

'In my dream. I did everything I could to wake up and I was held just like this, hands behind my back, against the wall.'

The demolition team comes through the door, laughing, holding tea, sledgehammers and machinery that looks like it'd be good for destroying a house made of stone. It'd look like a fun job if she weren't imagining them blithely swinging the hammer at her head.

'Help!' Tanya cries out.

'They won't be able to hear you, I've told you,' Amira says. 'How did I do it in your dream?'

'You just spoke to me and I woke up.'

'I'm speaking to you now. That doesn't seem to be working,' Amira says.

'You're getting facetious, you know,' Tanya says. 'I like it.'

'You bring it out in me. My sister did as well.'

'Wait,' Tanya says. 'That's it.'

'What?'

'You saw your sister just now. She faded away but you were able to touch hands, really briefly.'

'I've never been able to do that before,' Amira says, 'I've never been close enough, she's always a corridor away.'

'And everything else you've touched, the nightmares, they turn to dust if you touch them.'

Amira nods. 'It's why there are piles of dust everywhere: I've got a lot of nightmares. How does that help?' she asks.

A radio is switched on in the corner. Tea is drained. Some of the men go upstairs. Work's about to start. One of them slams a hammer into the wooden railing on the landing. Spindles fall.

'Careful,' one of them says, 'I've got to go up there. Oliver said there might be valuable stuff left, not that I'll hand it over, he's not paying enough. This place gives me the willies. I don't fancy being left upstairs without a staircase. You can smash it as much as you like after.'

The ivy shivers around them. The house is watching the unbuilders, waiting, worrying.

'I've got a hypothesis,' Tanya tries to say. A tendril has encircled her neck and is squeezing breath and words out of her. She twists her hands in their ivy handcuffs. They've loosened, as she'd hoped. The house must be distracted again.

She can move her fingers just enough to reach part of the plant. The ivy recoils and contracts, pulling her against the wall for one moment, then turns to dust.

The workers look over at the big mound of dust on the floor, with two people-shaped dips in it.

'You see that, Danny?' one of them asks.

Danny nods, mouth open.

'Told you this house was weird.'

Danny nods again and looks around the house. 'Weeeeiirrrd,' he says, holding onto the middle of the word like it could protect him.

'I'm going upstairs to hit something,' the first man says.

Danny nods. He waits till his friend has gone up then points at the dust. 'Got my eye on you,' he says.

'What just happened?' Amira asks.

'Sometimes the dreams turn to dust and sometimes they don't. You shoved the girls who bullied me out of the way but they didn't turn to dust, and yet Charlie could turn his own nightmare self into ashes. It made me wonder if you can only get rid of something if it was your own nightmare. So, as I'd dreamt about being suffocated by ivy, I thought it might work.'

'And it did,' Amira says. She pauses. 'But why was I able to touch Yana? She's in my dreams, my life, not yours. I didn't turn her to dust.'

'I don't know. Maybe it's because she's your good dream,' Tanya says gently. 'You don't need to get rid of her.'

Amira just sits there, a smile growing on her face. 'She is. She's my good dream,' she says.

Tanya stands, brushing herself as best she can but the dust clings to the webbing. Noticing them, Danny the builder runs for the door. 'Ghosts!' he shouts.

Upstairs, a sledgehammer finds wall. Wailing fills the house. It's been wounded.

The scuttling goes off upstairs. It's accompanied by a scraping sound, like teeth against bone.

A man screams. There's a thud. He sprints down the stairs. 'Get out,' he screams. 'GET OUT NOW!' His arm is bleeding heavily. Workers emerge from different rooms, carrying tools or furniture.

'What is it, mate?' one asks.

'Can't say,' he says. 'Wouldn't know where to start, mate. I'm off, you can stay here if you like but I wouldn't advise it.' He leaves at a run. Another follows. Shouts come from upstairs, followed by a man half-falling down the stairs. He doesn't even stop to say anything before running out of the front door.

Tanya moves towards them, drawing their attention. She waves to them. She must look like a walking, waving dust statue.

If they notice her, it only confirms their worst suspicions. The builders run and carry on running. Mr Oliver is going to have to find more staff.

Tanya runs to the dining room. Miss Quill is still lying on the floor. Tanya kneels down, feels for a pulse. It's faint.

'We should leave,' Amira says. 'The door's wide open but the house won't be distracted for long.'

'You go,' Tanya says. 'Call for an ambulance but get out of the house. Miss Quill will be OK until the paramedics arrive. I'm going up there.' She points up the stairs.

'You've been trying to get out all night!'

Tanya brushes more dust and webbing off. 'There's something in this house, other than the nightmares it makes. If I don't find out what it is, I'll keep coming back here, even when it's demolished. I'll be like Alice, with a face but without a stone house.'

'You could get injured,' Amira says, grabbing her hand and pulling her towards the door. 'Please. We can come back with other people later.'

Tanya resists, taking her hand away. 'Call an ambulance and the police. Get the neighbours, anyone, tell them we're here.'

She turns and walks up the stairs. She doesn't look back. Time to see what the stone house is hiding.

CHAPTER FORTY

THE ANSWER

Tanya grips the banister as she climbs. The house is quiet, listening to her every step.

On the top floor, she waits. Listens back.

TAP TAP TAP. Scuttle.

It's in Amira's bedroom.

You can do this, Tanya tells herself. She opens the door. Something is in the centre of the room.

It's huge and white. Curled up like a skeletal fist that takes up most of the room.

It raises its head. A cluster of eight white eyes holds her gaze. It's a spider. Made of bleached bone. Unlike other spiders, it has eyelids. They close with a bone tick like a myriad china dolls' eyes. Its legs click out, one by one, until all eight of them stand high above her, slightly bent at their knees, ready to pounce.

Downstairs, the front door slams. Amira must have left. Tanya's alone. She wishes she wasn't.

The bone spider's fangs appear. Bright bone chiseled into sharp points. The creature screeches, rearing above her.

This wasn't her nightmare before.

It is now.

Tanya runs.

CHAPTER FORTY-ONE

WAKING UP

Miss Quill opens her eyes. Alan is crouched down next to her. Panic on his face. 'I thought I told you to stay where you were,' she says.

'I saw Amira here running out. She told me you needed help,' he says. Amira is standing next to him, she steps forward.

Miss Quill tries to get up. Her whole body aches.

'You should take it slowly,' he says. 'I don't know how long you were unconscious.'

'Where's Tanya?' Miss Quill asks.

'She went upstairs and sent me to get help,' Amira says, walking towards the staircase. 'I shouldn't have gone.'

Something crashes into a wall upstairs. Tanya's yell for help echoes round the house.

Her footsteps sound like she's slipping down the top stairs. She appears on the first-floor landing, stumbling. 'Don't come up,' she shouts down to them. 'It's coming,' she says.

'What's coming?' Alan asks.

And then it appears. Two long, thin legs climb down the last stair onto the landing, followed by six more, attached to a large spider-creature made out of bones. It throws a loop of web around Tanya's running feet.

Tanya crashes into the banister. Some of the spindles are already missing but more fall onto the hallway floor. The banister makes a cracking sound. The spider moves towards her. Miss Quill looks around for anything they can use to stop it. There's nothing.

Tanya manages to stand, swaying on her bound feet.

The spider pounces on her.

Both of them crash through the railing, falling towards the hallway floor.

'No!' Amira cries out.

Silk threads hit the walls of the hall, a metre off the ground. The spider lands upon it, balancing on the threads as if on eight tightropes. It's wrapping Tanya up, mummifying her.

It stares down at Tanya's body. She isn't moving. Her face is frozen in terror.

The spider's blinks sound like a camera shutter as if it's taking a photo of its paralysed prey. It raises one spear-like leg and holds it above Tanya's heart.

Alan runs towards it. The creature turns from Tanya and hisses. It comes towards them. The spider's bone feet tap on the floor as if impatient. Alan picks up part of the broken railing and, raising it high, his arm shaking, he moves towards it. It flicks him away as if he were an insect.

He hits the wall. Miss Quill and Amira rush to help him up. 'I'm fine,' he says. 'We've got to stop it.'

The spider climbs back to Tanya in the web. Its fangs are out. Its bone feelers turn Tanya's head so that her neck is exposed.

'What are we going to do?' Amira asks desperately.

Miss Quill looks again around the room at the resources to hand. 'We're going to wrap it in its own web,' she says.

CHAPTER FORTY-TWO

ARACHNOPHOBIA

'We can use its own web to trap it,' Quill says.

'How?' Alan asks. He is still shaking. A bruise is already developing on his cheekbone.

'We need to make it into one long rope,' she replies. 'Alan, you bring the spider over here to distract it, and Amira and I will cut the web from the walls and twist it into one strong strand.'

'Do you think it'll work?' Alan says.

'If it doesn't, then you'll be the first to be eaten,' Miss Quill says calmly.

'That's reassuring,' Alan says, blinking.

Alan claps his hands. 'Hello there, um, spider,' he says, moving backwards very slowly.

The spider twists its head, watching him. The bone spider grabs Tanya under one leg and slowly steps off the web. It places her on the floor and stands in front of her, rearing up.

'That's it,' Alan says, his voice quavering. 'This way.'

Miss Quill hacks through where each strand of web is attached to the wall. When they all lie on the floor, Miss Quill and Amira roll it into one rope then hold an end each, like a game of Tug-of-War where they're on the same side.

'Walk behind it, then we'll cross over, being careful not to get tangled up ourselves,' Miss Quill says to Amira. 'The aim is to immobilize it by wrapping the web round its lowest knee joint. Keep back as far as you can.'

Amira and Miss Quill walk round and round the spider's back legs, crossing under each other's arms. Around them, the nightmares of the stone house form a circle. The spider is directing them, flicking its front legs like a general ordering an attack.

Miss Quill and Amira do their best to ignore them. Alan, though, hasn't seen his nightmares walking. An elderly man stands next to him. He's rasping, trying to talk.

'Dad?' Alan says, reaching towards him.

'Don't listen, Alan,' Miss Quill says. 'It's trying to distract us, which means we're winning.'

Alan nods, his eyes full of pain. He keeps glancing over to where his dad has slumped, clutching his chest.

'It's working,' Miss Quill says. The spider turns round and round to see what they are doing, getting itself further wrapped up. They work quickly until all eight legs have been wrapped several times. 'Now pull tighter,' Miss Quill says to Amira. Alan joins her to help.

The spider tries to rear up but can't lift its front legs off the ground. It surges forward but Amira and Alan pull tighter and it's forced into a corner, stuck fast in its own web. Its front legs buckling, it falls onto its knees. Lowering its head, it begins biting through the silk binding.

Miss Quill forces the web she's gathered into its mouthparts, twisting the gag into a sticky knot behind its head. It blinks at her rapidly, click, click, click as if remembering her face for a later attack. From behind the gag comes the sound of a strangled scream.

Amira runs to Tanya. 'You've got to help Tanya,' she says. 'Her face is turning blue.'

They crouch down next to Tanya's still body. 'Her circulation has been cut off,' Miss Quill says, sawing through the threads as quickly as possible.

'Wake up, Tanya,' Amira says, tears falling onto Tanya's face. 'Please. Wake up. This can't happen again.'

Miss Quill finishes cutting. Tanya lies motionless in her opened cobweb cocoon.

'Time to get up now, Miss Adeola. Break time's over,' Miss Quill shouts, slapping her face.

Tanya's eyelids flutter, ever so slightly.

'Breathe, Tanya,' Amira says. 'Please.'

The spider scratches at the floor behind them. Miss Quill checks. It can't move.

Tanya whimpers and tries to wriggle. She's stuck to the web. They peel the clinging silk from her clothes and skin. She sits up. 'Thank you,' she says. 'I thought that was it,' she says. 'Everything went fuzzy and dark.'

Amira leans over and hugs her tightly.

'I'm alright,' Tanya says. 'Really.'

Amira wipes away tears. She looks over to the spider. It's making a strange sound, like a chirrup, and trying to move its front legs. Above it, an image is forming.

'We need to wrap it up tighter,' Miss Quill says, 'it's trying to conjure more nightmares.' She places the penknife in her jacket pocket and gathers more webs from the walls.

Tanya walks slowly towards the spider. Above it, the faint image of another bone spider is forming. 'It's making another spider,' she says.

'If it can't attack us, it's sending a dream version,' Miss Quill says. 'As if *it* wasn't enough of a nightmare by itself. You're attacking the wrong people,' Miss Quill shouts at the spider.

The dream-spun spider is throwing a ball of web and scuttling after it. It fades in and out. Without free movement, the original bone spider doesn't seem able to sustain it.

The image of the dream spider is fading. The bone spider gives a muffled cry. Miss Quill wraps web around her open hands like a sticky cat's cradle. The bone spider blinks quickly. The dream version scuttles near, reaching out a leg to its creator. They touch.

Tanya walks behind Miss Quill and takes the penknife from her pocket. She runs to the spider.

'What are you doing? Get away,' Amira says.

'You can't kill it with that,' Miss Quill says.

'I'm not trying to kill it,' Tanya replies, taking the penknife towards the spider. She begins to cut through the web. 'I'm letting it go.'

'Stop it. Now!' Miss Quill shouts.

Too late. The front legs of the bone spider are free. It waves them in the air.

The image of the dream spider crystallises. It ticks across the floor on tiny bone legs, gathering its own thread into a larger ball. Throwing it into the air, it wiggles its abdomen and jumps on the ball as it lands.

'It's only a baby,' Alan says, his eyes wide.

It then picks up the cobweb ball and stands on its back legs. A larger dream spider appears, identical to the real one in front of them. It gathers the tiny one up. Their bones scrape together.

'It's a parent and child,' Tanya says. She points to the real bone spider in the corner. 'I think that's her child.'

The image fades and is replaced by the hall they're standing in. In the centre of the room is a rectangular black box. The baby bone spider scuttles up the side, making a squeaking sound, and drops down into the box. Two men in black come in and close the box. They carry it out on their shoulders. It's a coffin.

The bone spider reaches towards the coffin. The vision turns to dust, covering the spider.

'Bloody hell,' Tanya says.

'It lost its baby?' Alan says.

'Maybe,' Miss Quill replies, inclining her head and staring at the bone spider. 'Maybe it's making the nightmares as retaliation.'

Tanya moves to within touching distance of the bone spider.

'Get away, Tanya,' Miss Quill calls.

The bone spider raises its front legs and places them either side of Tanya's neck.

'Don't anyone move,' Tanya says. Her voice is tight and breathless. She holds herself stiffly.

The spider's bone legs turn Tanya around. Its eyes scan her. It blinks, sounding like eight teacups chinking on their saucers. Its legs fold back and one dips below the other as it lowers its head.

'Did that spider just bow?' Alan says. He'll need years of therapy for all this.

'I don't think it's trying to hurt us,' Tanya says, turning round.

'How can you say that?' Miss Quill says, so angry her voice comes out even more sharp and pointed. 'It practically threw you off the landing.'

'Or I fell and it caught me, wrapping me so I wouldn't hit the floor,' Tanya says. 'You said it was attacking the wrong people. I think *we've* got it wrong.'

The bone spider curls up as best it can in its own web.

'It was trying to comfort itself with a dream of its child that then turned into a nightmare,' Tanya says. 'What if it does the same to anyone who comes here? It could be trying to comfort scared children like me. It might even see us all as children.'

'Or it's luring people into its web with dreams in order to wrap them up and eat them,' Miss Quill says, folding her arms. 'If you let it out and it attacks, then I'll hold you responsible.'

'If you let it out and it attacks, then we'll all be slowly decomposing in a cobweb coffin,' Tanya says. '"I told you so" is hardly going to be the worst thing. On the other hand, we could be detaining a harmless creature.'

Outside, a motor starts chugging. Alan peeks through the window. 'Uh oh,' he says.

'What is it?' Tanya asks.

'I don't suppose any other houses in the road are up for demolition?' he asks.

'Not that we know of,' Miss Quill replies.

'Then it looks like the wrecking ball is for us,' he says.

CHAPTER FORTY-THREE

THE BONE SPIDERS

'What's going on?' Tanya asks.

'According to Mr Oliver,' Miss Quill says, 'the demolition begins this afternoon. Clearly they're getting ready.'

'Mainly by eating sandwiches,' Alan says, still looking out. 'And drinking tea.'

'I thought we'd scared them away,' Tanya says.

'I've met Constantine Oliver,' Miss Quill says. 'He'll have forced them back or hired new workers. He wants this place knocked down today.'

'We can't let them knock it down,' Tanya says. 'It lives here.'

'We don't know *what* it does or why it's here,' Miss Quill says. 'You came here to find Amira, you found her;

251

I came here to find you, here you are. Now we go. If I'm found here, I'm in significant trouble.'

'But it's lost its baby. We can't leave it like this.' The bone spider gently touches Tanya's shoulder with its front legs. Without thinking, she puts out a hand. They touch. Warm flesh and cold bone. She starts hacking though the rest of the web that ties its legs together.

'It's not our business,' Miss Quill says, folding her arms.

'Not our business?' Tanya says. 'Do you think we've found a new earth species here, or do you think it could possibly have fallen through the Rift at some point?'

'Of course it isn't from Earth,' Miss Quill says.

'Then do you think we should let a nightmare-creating alien loose in London when its home has been destroyed?' She frees another of the spider's legs and stares at Miss Quill.

Miss Quill stares back. There's a glint in her eye, as if enjoying the challenge. She looks down at her watch. 'Then we'd better start looking for its offspring, I suppose.'

Tanya slices the spider out of the last of its cuffs. It bows again. She finds herself bowing back.

The spider's legs click together. Tanya's mum, a floating molasses cake, her dad smiling, Tanya being buried in her father's grave. Each image lingers then fades.

'It's spinning dreams like a web,' Tanya says. 'I don't think it knows the difference between good dreams and nightmares.'

As it weaves the dreams, it looks around the room and other images appear. Corridors and screams and –

'That is quite enough, thank you,' Miss Quill says to the spider.

'In its dream it showed its baby climbing into a coffin. What if it was Alice's? She died last year,' Tanya says, running towards the stairs. 'We have to find out where she was buried. I found a load of papers in the attic. Something up there could help.'

Halfway up the stairs, she looks down at them all staring up at her. 'Well, come on then. There are a LOT of documents to get through. Oh, and be careful walking across the landing. Someone broke the railing.'

CHAPTER FORTY-FOUR

THE PAPERS

Tanya looks down from the attic. Miss Quill, Amira and Alan look up at her. 'Promise you won't go anywhere?' she says.

'Absolutely,' Miss Quill says. 'But if we have to go, we'll leave the spider as your babysitter, seeing as you think it perfectly safe.'

'Just stay there, would you?' Tanya says, jumping across the slats to the boxes of documents. She tries to lift it. Far too heavy, instead she pulls at the cardboard the box is resting on. The cardboard tears away, leaving the box where it is.

'Change of plan,' Tanya says, popping her head back out the door. 'I'll pass big piles of paper down.'

Miss Quill shrugs. She's standing at the front window, watching the workers. 'You'd better hurry. I think they're threatening to finish their tea. It won't matter once a large metal ball is swinging towards the house.'

'But you said it was this afternoon,' Tanya says.

'I said that Constantine Oliver told me it was this afternoon. Hardly a reliable source.'

Tanya scoops up a thick layer of papers and hands them to Alan who's waiting at the top of the stepladder. She goes back, grabs some more and repeats till they yell at her to stop. Amira sits cross-legged on the floor, going slowly through her pile; Miss Quill and Alan have a bed each to work on. Miss Quill has laid hers out systematically; Alan, not so much.

Tanya stays in the attic. It feels different up here now, as does the whole stone house. The cobwebs, either thrown up by the spider or one of its tiny, non-bony relatives, now feel like the tie-dyed sheets her aunt swagged up on the lounge ceiling 'to make it cosy'. She sits on a dusty blanket and reads documents by torchlight. Most of them are Alice's old bills and bank statements. Many of the bills were red ones, which is odd because most of the bank statements showed a ridiculously healthy balance that kept going upwards due to interest rates that Tanya hadn't known went that high. Alice had hardly spent anything, other than on bills and deliveries of tinned orange food.

A door slams downstairs. Heavy, booted steps cross the hallway, louder than the click-click of the spider's spinnerets.

'They're coming back in,' Tanya says.

'What should we do?' Alan asks.

'Keep going,' Miss Quill says.

'They won't find us easily,' Amira says. 'The bone spider is throwing its fine web over us.'

'Like an invisibility cloak?' Alan says. Tanya can hear the geek in his voice from up here. She smiles. She's the same.

'If they properly search in here, though, they'll find us,' Amira says.

'We can scare them first though, right?' Alan asks.

'Absolutely,' Miss Quill says. There's something in her voice, too – Tanya can hear it. It might even be a smile.

For the next half an hour, the shuffling of paper, the occasional sigh and the tapping of the bone spider's legs is all that can be heard. Tanya, having gone through her first pile of documents, takes out a shoebox covered in decoupage flowers: forget-me-knots, dandelions, roses.

As she opens an envelope, Alan whispers up to her, 'I've got something that could be useful.'

257

Tanya moves across the beams then lies flat out along the cardboard, looking down at them through the hatch. She waves at Amira.

'What've you got?' Tanya asks.

'Ssh,' says Miss Quill, 'keep your voice down, would you? Do you want us to be found?'

Alan holds up a plastic folder. 'A file of documents from around the time of Alice Parsons' death. I've found a copy of her death certificate and a list of instructions to the undertaker.' He keeps his voice very quiet.

'What's on the list?' Tanya whispers back.

'She wanted an open casket wake in this house, but nobody was to be invited.'

'I like the sound of Alice,' Miss Quill says.

'After the funeral, her coffin was to be taken to the family vault in Kensal Green cemetery, the tomb to be left open due to her long-term fear of premature burial.'

'Very sensible,' Miss Quill says, nodding.

'How is that, in any way, sensible?' Tanya says.

'If you're ever buried ten metres underground on a hostile planet with only a toothpick and a straw to save you, you'll know how stupid that question is.'

Tanya shakes her head. 'Anything else, Alan?'

He looks down the list. 'She wanted flowers from the garden on top of the coffin and, now this *is* interesting, she asks if they can locate her daughter, Sophia, to inform her of Alice's death. There's an asterisk there, and underneath a note saying "delicacy is required as my daughter does not know me". And a key, to the vault maybe.'

'That's so sad. So she did have a daughter,' Tanya says. She thinks of all those dolls in the room of unblinking eyes.

'It says here the daughter was adopted,' Alan continues. 'There's a certificate attached. "Unwed", it says. Alice Parsons gave birth to a baby girl, Catherine Grace Parsons, November 11, 1959. Catherine was adopted by a couple from Stoke Newington. They may have changed her name afterwards.'

Miss Quill's phone rings. It's Charlie. 'Yes, yes, of course I'm fine,' she whispers. 'We've found Tanya. And a dream-making alien spider.' She pauses, listening. 'No, you don't need to come. Yes, really. Now go and amuse yourselves until we get back.'

Footsteps tramp up the stairs. 'Did you hear a mobile go off?' one of the workers shouts.

'Keep the noise down, will you?' Tanya whispers to Miss Quill. 'Do you want us all to be found here?'

'Shut up,' Miss Quill replies. Tanya retreats into the attic.

The men walk down the corridor towards them. 'Could've sworn I heard a ringtone up here,' he says.

'That's the least of it, Doug. I wouldn't have come back but he told me I wouldn't be paid at all if I didn't. I saw some weird stuff earlier. From what I heard, something dodgy happened here,' a second man says.

'What, like a murder or something?' Doug says.

'Yeah. Or worse.'

'Worse than murder?' Doug doesn't sound convinced. Tanya sticks her head out of the hatch and pulls a face at Amira.

'Alright, maybe not worse, but really bad. I can't even tell you what I saw.'

'Have you been through everything up here?' Doug says.

'Don't know if there's any point. I've searched downstairs and there's nothing we can sell. There's a load of creepy dolls that I wouldn't give to a charity shop and a TV that hasn't been turned on since 1985.'

'I know the feeling.'

They're standing right outside the slightly open door. Tanya lifts her head back up. They walk in. She closes her eyes, as if that'll help in any way at all.

'I mean, look what's in here,' Doug says. 'Dodgy old furniture that'll collapse if we move it, filled with an old woman's knickers. Not my idea of fun. Anyway, once Oliver gets here, it won't matter. He'll give the nod and this house'll be a pile of smashed stone before dinnertime.' His voice fades slightly as if he's turning away.

Footsteps back out onto the hallway floorboards. The door closes.

'Right,' Tanya says, head popping out of the attic again like an upside down whack-a-mole. 'We don't have much time. Someone needs to stay here to look after the bone spider and work out where we can relocate her.'

'Where would that be?' Alan asks.

'No idea,' Tanya says. 'Nightmares aren't welcome anywhere.'

'And where are you going?' Miss Quill asks.

'I'm going to find a baby bone spider,' Tanya says. 'Who's going to drive me?'

'I will,' Alan says, standing up.

'Do you want to come too?' Tanya asks Amira.

Amira shakes her head and looks back down to the papers on her lap.

'OK, then,' Tanya says. 'But you should both look out for Constantine Oliver and his wrecking ball.'

CHAPTER FORTY-FIVE

THE LOST LETTERS

Tanya sits in the front of Alan's Mini. The box of letters is on her lap.

'Do you think Amira'll be okay?' she asks.

'Why wouldn't she be?' Alan asks, eyes on the road. He flinches as a lorry drives past.

'She doesn't know Miss Quill. And you know how she can be quite…'

'Brusque? Sharp? Rude?' he says. Each of the words brings a bigger smile to his face. 'She doesn't mean it really.'

'She doesn't?' Tanya says, incredulity soaked into her voice like rum in black fruitcake.

'Oh no. It's just her way,' Alan says.

'Have you seen her any other way?' Tanya asks. Maybe she acts differently with other adults, on her own. Maybe she's let Alan in on a different Quill.

'Oh no,' Alan says. 'That would be strange.'

Poor Alan.

Alan squints at a road sign. He's gone the wrong way already. 'Amira will be safe with Miss Quill. I don't know much about what's happened to her, but the stone house has been her refuge for the last weeks. It's probably the safest place she's been in for a long time.'

'Even with the nightmares?' Tanya asks.

'We carry our nightmares with us,' Alan says. 'The spider spins them outside of your body, but they're still there, walking behind you wherever you go.'

'I'm so glad you said you'd take me, Alan,' Tanya says, looking out of the window. 'You're a ray of hope in a dark, dark world.'

'Thank you,' he says shyly. She's glad now that he didn't pick up on the sarcasm.

They've hit a traffic jam. It feels like the Mini is moving an inch at a time. Tanya opens the box of letters and looks inside the top envelope. She reads through it in silence then breathes out when she reaches the end. She flicks through all the envelopes in the box.

'They're letters Alice wrote to her daughter. Never sent.' She feels like crying. The tale of several lives in a sorrow of letters.

'What does the first one say?' Alan asks.

'I'll read it out,' Tanya says. She composes herself then begins.

My daughter, my darling Catherine,
Happy Birthday!

It's been ten years since I saw your face but I remember it as if you were next to me now. Your hair was so black. Your eyes were bright blue, but I've been told that babies' eyes change in the first weeks of their lives. They could be brown now. I remember your little fists held up to your chin and your tiny lips blowing bubbles.

I was told that it was a bad idea to have a photograph, as it would cause me to have more of an attachment to you. I wish I hadn't listened. Please believe me, Sophia, I wish I hadn't listened to any of them. If I had a photo of you as you are now, I'd look at it every day and think of you. I don't know your face, you see. I've heard friends say about their children they were allowed to keep, that they have 'their nose' or 'their eyes' but I'd never say that about you. You have your nose and your eyes. I wouldn't recognise you if I saw you in the street. Secretly, though, I hope you'll look up one day and see me in the window. Or I'll look up one day and see you in yours. And we'll know.

This is your birthday. I can't help imagining what you're doing, who you're with. I made you a cake! I had the ingredients sent here as I don't like to go out, just in case you come to find me. I know it's silly, but waiting for you is the least I can do. The cake is on the dining-room table, where I've put all the comics I'm keeping for you. A real sweep. All these characters and heroes swing through my letterbox every week and I pretend I'm reading to you even though you might be a bit grown up for that now.

I have a house! Your Nonna and Grandpops left this house to me but I still can't forgive them. If you find me, then there'd be plenty of room for you. You can pick your own room, of course, but there's one that I'm reserving for you. It's on the top floor and looks out over both the front and back gardens. You can see miles of sky in that room. It was Bonfire Night last week and I opened the window and watched as fireworks squealed across the night, writing their signatures in bright ink and smoke. I know you'd have loved it. In those last days of my pregnancy, I went to a Guy Fawkes' Night and you wriggled around and turned inside me like a Catherine Wheel. That's when I gave you your name. I don't even know if that's your name any more, but you will always be Catherine to me.

Happy birthday again, darling Catherine
  Your mum,
  Alice
  Xxx

Alan rubs his knuckle under his eye, removing a tear. They don't speak for a few minutes.

'Hell,' says Tanya, at last.

'Yeah,' Alan says.

'There's more,' Tanya says, looking through them all. None of them has been opened, none sent to the adoption agency on the envelope. How was Catherine supposed to find Alice if she'd never received them?

'I'm not sure we should be looking at them,' Alan says. 'It feels too private.'

'But what if we can help?' Tanya says. 'Maybe we can find Catherine, or whatever her name is now.'

'Adoption or family break-up is very complex,' Alan says. 'It's not going to be a case of Happily Ever After. Alice won't get her reunion.' He looks older suddenly, as if pain had moved in.

'If I can help a family get back together, even if it's after someone's died, then I will,' Tanya says.

'Are you sure this is about Alice and Catherine?' Alan asks gently.

'Who else would I be talking about?' she asks, then, quickly, before he can answer, continues. 'She talks about the bone spiders here. That might be able to help us.'

Dearest Catherine,

Something amazing has happened. It's not your birthday yet, but I had to write and tell you. Are you afraid of spiders? I hope not. I've always liked them. They keep flies away and help me feel I'm not alone. I thought I'd seen really big spiders, until last week. Remember me telling you that I couldn't keep up with the cobwebs any more, and that I'd been having really bad dreams? Turns out it wasn't my illness. It was the Bone Spider. I caught her reflection in the television screen and screamed. She scuttled away, legs scrabbling on the floor like running knitting needles.

I went looking for her but she must have covered herself. She can weave webs that hide her, and anyone she chooses to. It came in very handy when that developer came round, Mr Oliver. His face is so smooth I'm surprised that smile of his doesn't fall right off. I watched him look through all the windows and then let himself in the back. He walked around the house like I'd agreed to sell and move into one of his nursing homes, instead of telling him to go away. Only I wasn't that polite.

I'm getting ahead of myself. I don't get to talk very much, you see. I kept an eye out for the next few days, and had pretty much decided I'd imagined her, when I lost my footing on the rug at the top of the stairs and fell. I hit a few of the steps and then found I was suspended in the air between the wall and the banister. I was cradled in a web. Standing at the bottom of the stairs was a huge spider with a distended abdomen, shining white and blinking at me. This arachnid made of bone had saved me from breaking all of mine.

She helped me get out, biting through the web. When I was free, she ran into the corner, head lowered. I walked over and thanked her, touching one of her shoulders. I'm not saying I wasn't scared, I thought my heart would explode.

She then raised her front legs and you appeared. You were crying in your cot and stopped when you saw me. You smiled, your little cheeks lifting. It was wonderful and terrible. It is the Bone Spider's gift to me. I believe she thinks she's helping. She helps me dream of you all the time, which always makes me happy and always makes me sad.

The Bone Spider makes the strangest of companions but that suits me. We even talk, in a way. Yesterday, I asked where she was from, and she started scratching on the hallway floor.

I tried to stop her, 'That's good wood,' I said, then realised that she was sketching. Using her legs as pairs of compasses, she drew circles within circles. When she'd finished, she led me up onto the landing. I looked down and saw she'd drawn a star system completely unlike ours. She pointed to a tiny planet on the outer corners and blinked at me. I didn't think spiders can cry but it looked to me as if they can.

You probably think I'm mad. I think I'm mad, but at least I get to dream of you when I'm awake.

All my love
Your Mum
Xxx

'A star system,' Tanya says, feeling stupid, and she doesn't like feeling stupid. 'Of course it is.'

'It's not the first thing you'd think of,' Alan says.

'The Bone Spider must have got here through the Rift,' Tanya says.

'Through the what?' Alan looks worried now.

'It's a… Never mind.'

'What about refusing to sell to Constantine Oliver?' Alan says. 'How did he get hold of the house?'

Tanya skims through the previous letter but there's nothing about Oliver. Then she reads the last one.

Dearest Catherine

Happy Birthday!

You're 55 today! I bet you've become a wonderful, kind, clever woman who doesn't allow anyone to push her around. I hope so. I wish that for you.

I didn't make you a cake this year, I'm so sorry. It's the first time I haven't. I was so tired this morning that I couldn't even face mixing the ingredients. Please forgive my laziness. I've lit a candle, though, placed it by the window in your room, and peeled back the cobwebs so that I can look out. There are celebratory fireworks tonight. They go on for weeks these days. Autumn skies remind me of you: the scent of sulphur and woodsmoke; fireworks that look like dandelion clocks.

I think this will be my last letter. I'm weak and finding it hard to get around the house. I'm not worried about me, it's what'll happen to the Bone Spiders that keeps me awake at night.

There are two now, did I tell you? One day she went down into the basement and stayed there for days. I went down and found an egg sac in her web. She must have been pregnant when she arrived. Weeks later, she came upstairs accompanied by a tiny spider, its spindly body made out of bones.

Since welcoming the Bone Spiders, the stone house has come alive. I'm going to change my will, asking that the house be kept as it is for a year so that the spiders will be safe, then given to a charity for refugees. If you ever find these letters, I hope you understand. Bet Constantine Oliver won't like that. He keeps coming round but I'm not letting him get his hands on this place. It's a shame I won't get to see him lose his smile.

The fireworks have stopped for tonight but they'll be back tomorrow. I wanted you to know that I'm not alone. The baby is learning to spin dreams like her mother and, in return, I sing it lullabies. It crawls into my lap and chirrups as I sing.

The mother Bone Spider knows what I want – she'll make sure that the last face I see is yours. I hope you're happy, my darling. I wish that for you always, and that you find something that brings you as much happiness as you have brought me.

With so much love, always
Mum
Xxx

Tanya and Alan are silent, taking it all in. 'She never sent them,' Tanya says, 'all those words and feelings and Catherine never knew.'

'We should tell Miss Quill about the change in will,' Alan says. 'If there's a way we can stop the demolition…' He trails off.

Tanya gets out her phone. It's on red. She knew she should've listened to April and charged it up, not that she'll tell her that.

'What is it?' Miss Quill answers with a hiss-whisper.

'Alice wanted the house to go to a charity for refugees,' Tanya says. 'There must be something in the documents that can prove it.'

'How do you know?'

'From her letters. She hated Constantine Oliver and wanted to protect the Bone Spiders.'

'We haven't got time to go through everything,' Miss Quill says. 'More builders have arrived. Oliver will turn up soon.'

'Just try,' Tanya says, then hangs up.

CHAPTER FORTY-SIX

THE VAULT

Tanya and Alan walk in silence through Kensal Green cemetery. Ornate grey-green tombs contrast with a bright blue sky. Headstones lean and list in the grass like time-frozen wildflowers.

Alice's family vault is in the second park. It's a large tomb with four crying stone women holding the roof up with their heads. Alan takes out the key. 'Let's see if this works,' he says.

The door opens. As they enter the tomb, the temperature drops. It takes a while for their eyes to adjust to the lack of light. Cobwebs are strung like bunting. Coffins and sarcophagi are tucked into the walls on their own shelves, with spaces left for future generations. In the centre sits a large stone table with a tomb bearing the name of the most recent interment. Alice.

The lid is slightly askew, showing a glimpse into the darkness inside. They heave the lid to one side. Alice's body lies on red velvet. Her bones and some flesh remain. Alan looks away.

'I can't see the little bone spider,' Tanya says, swallowing down disgust and guilt at her disgust.

Alan shines his torch into each compartment. 'Nothing in here,' he says. 'Only dust.'

'That could mean it's here,' Tanya says.

'Or maybe we're in an old tomb,' Alan says. 'You'd expect dust and lots of cobwebs.'

'Even if it's in here,' Alan says, 'how are we going to get it to come out?'

'We should sing,' Tanya says, remembering the letters. 'Alice sang to it. Do you know any lullabies?'

'I'm not the best singer,' Alan says.

'I don't think that matters,' Tanya replies. A memory comes back, like a Bone Spider spun dream, of her dad singing "Rock-a-bye Baby". 'I'll start.'

The sound of singing, with Alan murmuring along, fills the cold vault. When they stop, it echoes. Nothing happens.

'Maybe it prefers different music. How's your jazz?' Tanya says.

'I'm more of a prog person,' Alan says.

Tap tap tap.

The very faintest sound comes from under the lowest shelf.

Alan gets onto his knees and presses his ear to the ground, looking underneath. 'I can see something,' he says. He gently raps on the shelf. Tap tap tap.

There's a pattering sound, and then the little Bone Spider appears. It sees Alan and scuttles back under the shelf.

Alan sings softly and Tanya joins in. Seconds later, it comes back out again.

'Hello, little one,' Alan says.

The Bone Spider blinks at him.

'We're here to take you back to your mum,' he says.

It drums all of its legs on the cold floor in turn.

Tanya kneels down and sketches the mother Bone Spider in the dust. It turns to Alan. Alan nods and smiles. The little Bone Spider then leaps onto his shoulder. It waves its front legs, then closes its eyes.

Images of Miss Quill begin to coalesce above Alan's head.

CHAPTER FORTY-SEVEN
THE RECKONING

Everything's gone quiet outside. To Miss Quill, silence does not mean peace; it means that war is about to begin. She places the document inside a folder and walks over to the front window. Constantine Oliver stands in the wreckage of the front garden, waving his expensively suited arms.

He's handed a hard hat. Another bad sign. Oliver walks towards the house.

'Stay here,' Miss Quill says to Amira and the Bone Spider. She marches out of the door, brushing the protective web from her suit. This is not the time to be invisible.

Constantine Oliver stands in the downstairs hallway. 'I can't wait to see this come crashing down,' he says, looking around the stone house with disgust.

'You will be waiting a very long time,' Miss Quill calls down. She walks across the landing.

'What an enormous pleasure,' Oliver says, his smile on full beam. 'You're not supposed to be here, are you, Miss Quill?'

'And neither are you, Mr Oliver,' Miss Quill replies. She holds up the document folder.

'I don't know what you're talking about,' he says, still smiling.

'Alice Parsons wanted the house to be used for refugees. She most definitely didn't want it going to you. I've got the evidence to prove it.'

'Miss Parsons' solicitor deals with her estate, it's nothing to do with me,' Oliver says, opening his hands out in a gesture of innocence.

'Funny, because I called Rajesh in your office. Yes,' she says, 'the one who gave in his notice today. He confirmed that you had received a copy of the amended will and, somehow, between you and Miss Parsons' solicitor, you managed to lose it.'

'That's slander,' he says. He has, however, become bone white.

'I intend to write it down, which would make it libel as well, were it not true. But it *is* true, isn't it?'

Oliver turns to look at his workers. They're all staring at him. 'Get out, all of you.' They trudge out, muttering about still being paid. Oliver takes out his phone. 'It'll take the police minutes to get here, Miss Quill,' he says.

'Good,' she says. 'I appreciate promptness.' She folds her arms. Upstairs, a scuttling sound is heard. 'I can't wait to tell them that you took a house from a dead woman against her explicit instructions while depriving the most vulnerable of a home. That's not going to look good for Constantine Oliver Ltd, is it? Not exactly "Serving the Community".'

Constantine Oliver slowly walks over. His face is centimetres from Miss Quill's. She can smell the bacon on his breath. 'You don't have a chance,' he says. 'I'll keep this wrapped up in legal issues until the estate has run out of money.'

'Maybe,' says Miss Quill, 'but you won't get your hands on the stone house till then.' The scuttling gets louder. It stops above their heads. The Bone Spider is on the landing.

Constantine Oliver's smile falls from his face and slides under the floorboards.

The Bone Spider jumps. It lands in front of Oliver and raises its front legs.

Thousands of tiny spiders appear, scuttling towards Oliver, climbing him, tapping their tiny legs on his face. He screams, scratching at his skin.

'Oh, I'm sorry,' Miss Quill says. 'Do you not like spiders? Are they your worst nightmare?'

Oliver runs for the door but it slams shut. Money spiders cover his face. He opens his mouth to shriek but the spiders run in, coating his tongue.

'Funny business to be in if you can't deal with spiders,' Miss Quill says.

Gurgling, Oliver drops to the floor. 'Please,' he whispers. His hands are covered in creeping web, sticking him to the floor like a trapped fly.

'I'm sure I can get the spiders to desist but you'll have to sign something first,' Miss Quill says. She takes a pen and notebook slowly out of her bag. 'I'll have to get our, sorry, *my* solicitor to make it official but I'm sure you'll sign then as well.'

He shakes his head. The spiders swing from his silver hair and try to prise open his eyes. 'Okay,' he splutters through a mouth full of dust and spiders.

'You'll sign?'

He nods. Miss Quill writes slowly, reading out loud: 'I, Mr Constantine Oliver, of Constantine Oliver Ltd, declare that I have no legal right to the property and that all monies shall be returned to the previous occupant's estate. I am a shameful, despicable person and no designer suits, shoes or smile can hide it.' She pauses. 'That last bit might not stay but I want you to sign it anyway.'

She places the document in front of Oliver and frees his hand enough to hold the pen. He pauses. The Bone Spider taps her feet. The spiders move into his ear canal. His hand shaking, Constantine Oliver signs his name.

Miss Quill picks up the paper. 'Thank you, Mr Oliver. It's been an enormous pleasure. I won't keep you any longer.'

The Bone Spider hits her front legs together and the dream spiders jump off Oliver's back and face and limbs. The web holding him shrinks. He scrambles up and runs for the now open door, tearing at his suit and screaming.

The dream spiders settle at the Bone Spider's feet and then fade.

Amira walks in. 'What happened?' she asks.

'Turns out Oliver has arachnophobia,' Miss Quill says. 'Even monsters have nightmares.'

CHAPTER FORTY-EIGHT

REUNION

'Where are all the builders?' Alan asks Tanya as they walk up to the stone house. There's no one in the front garden, no sign of builders drinking tea or smashing stone.

'They could be round the back?' Tanya says.

'Doesn't sound like it,' Alan says. He looks down at the shoebox in his hand as if worried he could drop it.

April and Ram are walking up the road towards them; Charlie and Matteusz a conspicuous distance behind.

Miss Quill emerges out of the stone house. 'What are you all doing here?' she says. 'I thought you didn't want anything to do with me.'

'We thought we'd ensure you were not hurt,' Matteusz says. Charlie nods once, imperiously, although he doesn't quite look Miss Quill in the eye.

'And what about you?' Miss Quill asks Ram. 'I suppose Miss MacLean persuaded you. Again.'

'I wouldn't say that,' Ram says.

'I'm surprised you're allowed out,' Miss Quill says to April.

'As you said, I'm very persuasive.'

'You'd better all come in then,' Miss Quill says. 'If you can bear being near each other for five minutes.'

The Bone Spider is in the lounge. She takes up almost all of the space. Amira is in the corner armchair. The others crowd around the doorway.

The Bone Spider starts to cover itself with the protective web.

'It's OK,' Tanya says. 'They're friendly – ish.' She takes the shoebox from Alan, places it on the floor and lifts the lid. A little bone leg appears. The Bone Spider chirrups and moves towards the box. The baby Bone Spider looks up at its mother and blinks. It climbs out, legs folding out like the spines of a tiny umbrella.

The little Bone Spider dances under her mother, rearing up and reaching for her. The mother nods to her, tasting her. Their chirruping sounds like singing.

The baby bumbles out from underneath her mother's thorax and runs to each one of them, jumping up to their knees.

'She's cute,' April says, bending and tickling the little Bone Spider under what could be a chin. 'Like a terrier.'

'Just don't throw her a bone,' Ram says. 'Don't think that would go down very well.'

The little Bone Spider runs back to its mum and leans against her.

The mother waves her legs and images appear of the little Bone Spider trapped in a coffin. The little one makes a keening sound and hides under its mother's leg. Its mother blinks and the nightmare stops, replaced with images of purple skies and caves full of webs. The baby opens one eye, then the other. It starts chirruping again.

'Do you think that's their home planet?' April asks.

'I'd say so,' Miss Quill says. 'Maybe they don't have nightmares there. They might teach each other the difference between bad dreams and good.'

'We should leave them to it,' Tanya says. 'I think we're intruding.'

CHAPTER FORTY-NINE

REFUGE AND REVENGE

It is strange and wonderful to step outside. The air smells of fresh grass and spilled petrol. Breathing it in feels like drinking water when thirsty. Everything seems so wide and open, even though I'm in a city where people are stacked on top of one another high up into the sky. My heart's beating too quickly. I have no idea what to do. It took so long to get here, and I lost so much. Now what?

'How can we help you now?' Tanya says. 'I'll do everything I can.'

'I want to go to the police,' I say.

Tanya nods. She squeezes my hand. 'Then I'm coming with you.'

* * *

The interview takes hours. First one officer asks me questions, then another asks me slightly different questions, then someone from immigration asks me more questions. I have one question I ask them, again and again: 'Do you know where my father is?' They don't seem to know, or want to tell me the answer.

It's twilight when I'm let out. Tanya is there with her mum and Miss Quill. I wonder what she's told her mum.

'You've told us where the smuggler lives,' one of the officers says. She has kind eyes. 'If we took you back to that street, do you think you could point out the house?'

I nod.

'You're sure you want to go?' Tanya asks, standing up.

'I think it'll help,' I say.

'Them or you?'

'Both, hopefully.'

'Then I'm coming with you,' Tanya says. Her mum shakes her head in exasperation but doesn't object.

Half an hour later, I point out the house with the whited-out windows. I can't believe I got so far that night. It was like the stone house, or the Bone Spider, called out to me. I'm glad that it did.

Six police officers line up outside the front door. One of them slams something into the front door and the others follow

*her in. Tanya and Miss Quill stand either side of me. We watch
as the man and his friends are brought out, their arms clamped
behind their backs. I don't cry until I see Zainer brought out.
And then I can't hold any of it back.*

*They've taken me back for more questioning. They're saying
words like 'definitely help your case' and 'brave journey' but
I'm tired. All I want is for the Bone Spider to wrap me up in
its invisibility web and for everyone to leave me alone.*

*The questions stop at last. The officer with the kind eyes
opens the door for me. I don't know where they're taking me
now.*

*Tanya and her mum are still there. They look as shattered
as I am. 'You should go home,' I say to them. 'Thank you so
much for…'*

*The kind officer nudges me. She points to the corner of the
reception where a tall, thin man stands, turning a hat in his
hands. It's Baba. He's crying. He runs to me and I jump at
him. He wraps me in his arms.*

CHAPTER FIFTY

THE STONE HOUSE

Three days later …

Tanya stands in the middle of the galaxy scratched on the hallway floor. The little Bone Spider scuttles from one planet to another, followed by her mother in a game of galactic chase. Above them all, the sky of their home planet is spun from their dreams.

Miss Quill walks in, bang on time. Alan follows behind her, scratching his head. 'Come on, then,' she says. 'Time to go.'

'Shouldn't we clear up?' Tanya says. 'Look.' She leads them through into the doll room. It's a mess. The cabinets have been carted off to the tip or an auction room, and the national dress dolls swept into a box in a

293

bright tangle of wrappers, bubas, saris, flamenco skirts and more.

'It's so sad,' Tanya says. Alice must have collected dolls for the daughter she never knew and who never came home, from countries she never visited, that only bore a vague relation to the dolls that represent them.

'I've been trying to contact Catherine,' Alan says, as if reading Tanya's mind.

'Any luck?' Tanya says.

'Not so far. I've hit a blank with the adoption agency.'

'What can I do?' Tanya asks. She wants to complete the circle. Weave everyone together.

'Even if we find her, she may not want to hear about her birth mother, remember that. You can't join everything up, Tanya.' Miss Quill touches Tanya's shoulder very briefly. 'You should know that.'

'Don't you think we should clear up in here, though?' Tanya says again.

'We'll leave it to the Bone Spiders to decide what to do with their house. We'll check in on them soon.'

The Bone Spiders are waiting by the door when they come out. 'Goodbye,' Tanya says. The little Bone Spider jumps onto her hand.

The mother Bone Spider walks across the hallway, her feet tick-tocking across the floor. She stops in front of them, bends her head and places one of her legs behind the other.

'How long do you think they can stay there?' Tanya asks, stopping in the garden and looking back. It's dusk. The stone house stands grey against a sky the colour of sherbet lollipops. A snail slowly climbs the railings.

'Well, we've got some news about that,' Miss Quill says. She nods to Alan.

Alan blushes. 'Felicity, Miss Quill's solicitor, has seen to it that Constantine Oliver has to return the money to Alice's estate. The evidence of a cover-up was overwhelming and he wasn't inclined to fight for some reason.'

'Fear is a powerful persuader,' Miss Quill says.

'You're a scary woman,' Tanya tells her.

'Thank you, Tanya,' Miss Quill replies, standing taller.

'Felicity, thanks to Miss Quill—'

'Don't bring me into it,' Miss Quill interrupts, bristling.

'Fine. Felicity, on behalf of Alice's estate, has appointed me caretaker for the house,' Alan says, smiling shyly, 'for at least a year, with a view to continuing when we find a charity to turn the stone house into a home for newly arrived refugees.'

'The Bone Spiders can stay here, spinning good dreams for residents,' Miss Quill says. 'Or, if they want to go home one day, I know someone who might take them. I've done some research and it looks like they're from a remote star system. They must've fallen through the Rift.'

'Until then, I'll be looking after the Bone Spiders,' Alan says.

'Felicity will be coming in to check up on you,' Miss Quill says. She's not looking at him.

'Really? Not you?' Alan asks, not looking at her.

'I'm a busy woman, Alan F. Turnpike, I may well be otherwise engaged on Thursday at half past seven. We'll have to see.'

Alan's grin gets bigger.

'Glad that's cleared up,' Tanya says. 'But there's one thing I haven't worked out. Why did I go to the stone house in the first place? What draws lonely people to it?'

'I would've thought that was obvious,' Miss Quill says. 'Dandelions.'

'Dandelions?'

'You said you blew on a dandelion clock that first day. Some of them stuck to you. There were more in the air, carried by the breeze. Some of *those* may have stuck to you.'

'So?'

'I thought everyone knew that they're homing beacons.'

'They are?'

'In many planets, people add a homing device to wind-wandering seeds.'

'The Bone Spider tried to bring her daughter back to the house by sending out the filamentous achenes?'

'Exactly. Only she found other lonely people instead,' Miss Quill says.

Tanya looks up to where she first saw Amira. Lit up by the lilac skies of a distant planet, the cobwebbed windows look like stained glass.

She picks the last dandelion clock in the garden and blows. Four o'clock. Not even close. The filamentous achenes catch a lift on the breeze and, hopefully, lead someone home.